❦

Elise was fairly certain that Maiju would invite her in to discuss all these marvelous ventures she should be trying. "Park it right in front," Maiju said. "Everyone's gone for the weekend. No one will care."

Elise pulled Maiju's car in front of the big brown-shingled Faculty House with its wide front porch. Maiju turned to her, her hand outstretched. Elise shook it awkwardly, feeling dazed.

Elise knew her eyes, never very guarded, had telegraphed her disappointment. She handed the car keys to Maiju and smiled at her. She felt brave, hopeful. She couldn't imagine waiting until tomorrow. Their eyes had locked. How long could they sit here gazing at each other before something happened? Elise felt— or was it only imagination?—that Maiju was leaning closer and closer. She could almost feel Maiju's breath on her cheeks. She sensed Maiju's hand beginning to rise, as if to touch Elise's breasts, or her lips…surely she wasn't imagining that, was she?

Elise

for P.E. and S.

THE FIRST OF THE ADELA HONEYCUTT CHRONICLES

Elise

CLAIRE KENSINGTON

spinsters book company

San Francisco

First edition
10-9-8-7-6-5-4-3-2-1

Spinsters Book Company
P.O. Box 410687
San Francisco, CA 94141

Copy editing by Ann Morse
Production: Joan Meyers
                 Pamela Ai Lin To
                 Kathleen Wilkinson
Text and cover design by Pam Wilson
Typeset by Joan Meyers in Palatino
Cover concept: P. Phung
Cover illustration: M. Tse

Printed in the U.S.A.

Library of Congress Cataloging-in-Publication Data
Kensington, Claire
    Elise/ by Claire Kensington. — 1st ed.
        p. cm. — (The Adela Honeycutt chronicles: bk 1)
    ISBN 0-933216-79-3 : $7.95
    I. Title. II. Series: Kensington, Claire. Adela
Honeycutt chronicles : bk. 1.
PS3561.E513E54   1991
813'.54—dc20   91-2044
                                                   CIP

This is a work of fiction. All references to actual people,
places, or situations are purely coincidental.

Chapter One

"Elise, honey, have you seen my panty hose?" Frances Gilready's smoky contralto echoed through the bathroom that connected her single room to Elise Lemoine's. Elise raised her head from the book she was reading and thought once again how she'd love to listen to Frances forever if only she didn't have to hear the words. "Honestly, babe," Frances was continuing, "I put them right on my bed and now I can't imagine where they've run off to."

Elise looked again at her book—*The Early Days of Theater in San Francisco*—with a hopeless roll of her eyes, for Frances would appear at her bathroom door in about...

"Elise! We've been back at school almost three days, and I've seen you twice for a grand total of a half-minute."

Elise smiled and turned to face her suitemate, who was about as unlike her in appearance as she could be. Elise's long, blunt-cut blond hair framed an oval face with defiant green-gold eyes mounted over prominent cheekbones; her skin was creamy smooth, as if she bathed in buttermilk. She was medium height and slender, though she felt positively plump compared to the modeling days of her early teens, when she'd subsisted for months on yogurt and diet colas.

Frances, by contrast, had the sort of dark auburn hair one mostly associates with beautiful horses, a wild spray of freckles across her nose, deep brown bedroom eyes, and a body that was classic in the '40s and '50s, too oom-pah-pah in the '60s and '70s, indolent in the '80s, but coming back into favor in the '90s. She could be alarmingly narcissistic, losing herself in the pleasure of stroking her own leg, while others got lost watching her. Elise and Frances vied for the title of the most beautiful woman on the campus of Adela Honeycutt College; they were also reputed to be among the wildest and most promiscuous.

"Well, *I've* been here," Elise noted. "It's you that's so busy." Her eyes twinkled as she watched the telltale slow grin spread over Frances's face.

"Indeed I am," Frances said. "After a summer spent in the boonies with my parents, I had to check in with my boyfriends, reclaim my territory, know what I mean? It's kind of like the dog who runs around lifting his leg on all the fire hydrants."

Elise snorted. "Lifting your hips, more like it. So you had a dull summer?"

Frances made a beeline for Elise's bed and threw herself on her back in one towering crash. "Relatively." That might mean anything, and Elise didn't really want to pursue it. She touched her pen to her lip as Frances stared back at her frankly. "Well, Elise, are you going to tell me your gossip or do I have to squeeze it out of you with a thumbscrew?"

Elise shrugged. "Nothing much. I stayed in San Francisco all summer with my parents."

"What about Jamie?"

Elise shook her head. "Jamie was in Virginia, thank god. I really didn't want to see her."

"Monica?"

Elise didn't answer. She turned back to her book.

Frances drummed her fingers on the metal bed frame. "Now listen, Elise Lemoine, even if your parents were sitting on top of you, you must have had some opportunity to tomcat around. Give."

6

Elise sighed. "Frances, did it ever occur to you that there might be something more to life than fucking?"

Frances stopped drumming and looked at Elise. "No, actually it hasn't. And it hasn't to you either. There's only one difference between you and me, babe, and that has to do with the object and not with the mania itself. So don't try to tell me you're something you're not."

She cast a sidelong glance at Elise, but Elise had rocked back in her desk chair so her face was hidden in shadow. She said nothing. Frances turned away, stretched, and began lightly running her fingers up and down the outsides of her thighs. "Oh, my, Elise, speaking of sexy women—have you seen that new professor from Yale or wherever she's from? My god, she's something, isn't she?" When still no answer came, Frances whipped her head around only to see Elise highlighting a section in her book with the chunky yellow pen. "Elise!"

"What, Frances? I have to work!"

"Have you checked out that new history teacher? She has a funny name...Maiju Rittola—"

"Mai-you," Elise corrected. "The 'j' in Finnish is pronounced like a 'y,' not an 'h.' "

"Finnish, huh? I always thought Finns were blond and strapping, like Swedes. This Maiju looks—well, almost exotic. But chilly, know what I mean? You'd need remote control to turn her on."

"I couldn't care less what she looks like," Elise said, annoyance sharpening her tone. "The administration switched me from Mr. Danielo to her for my independent study advisor. I went and yelled at them but they said tough luck."

Frances looked sympathetic. "What's your project again?"

"It's about Adela Honeycutt herself—how she started this place, who she was. Remember, the college was just given all her letters and diaries and papers. I spent the summer reading tons of stuff about theater in San Francisco in the late 1800s. You did know Adela was an actor, didn't you?"

"Of course," Frances said. "Who could miss it? The whole campus reeks of the the-a-tah."

7

"Well, the switch to Rittola sort of makes sense, since Danielo is literature and Rittola is history, but it really infuriated me because they didn't ask, for one thing, and I'd already talked to Danielo and set up a plan of action. Now I have to go over the same ground with Professor Rittola and maybe she'll want me to do something entirely different."

Frances winked at Elise. "Wait 'til you see her before you waste a lot of time complaining."

"For god's sake, Frances!" Elise exploded. "If you find her so attractive, maybe you should start barking up the other side of the tree."

Frances chuckled. "Oh no, honey, that's your territory. How could I hope to compete with the woman who single-handedly turned out a fifth of the freshman class?" She laughed at Elise's sour expression. "You were a sex fiend then, and you haven't changed an iota since, even though you're trying to kid yourself. And believe me, babe, Jamie isn't going to just disappear."

Elise dropped her forehead to the desk with a thunk. "Spare me," she moaned. "Frances, do me a favor, all right? I have no idea where your panty hose are, and I really need to read this material before I see Professor Rittola tomorrow. Let's make a lunch date for later in the week and then you can torment me all you want, okay?"

"Deal," Frances said. "Besides, I'm late myself." She flounced off the bed and disappeared into their shared bathroom, closing the door after her. Elise listened to the hairbrush catch and pull through Frances's heavy waves. Soundproofing in these nearly hundred-year-old dorms was chancy at best. Then the door opened again, as Elise knew it would. "Wish me luck, gorgeous. I'm going after a real winner this time."

"Married?"

"The best ones are, honey."

"Luck," Elise said. When the door closed again, she stared at her theater book, put it down, and crossed the room to root through a stack of photocopied pages from Adela Honeycutt's diaries. Elise had been arranging the sections by date, and now she took a page from deep in the pile, near the close of Adela's journal-keeping. As Elise began to read, she saw that she'd picked well, for Adela was describing the site for her future school:

"The Sacramento River runs like a swollen artery down the arm of California, emerging at the elbow to pour its strength into San Francisco Bay. But at the confluence of the river and the bay is a delicate and intricate series of canals and islands, where the arterial river becomes divided into hundreds of capillaries, where birds and fish and animals live in abundance, where the promise of spring turns into a hot, verdant summer, a languid fall, and a dripping winter...where young women could come and drink in the pleasures of nature rather than revel in what I now see are the cynical, jaded, and ultimately empty promises of life in San Francisco. It is at this confluence that I will found my college, my legacy, Adela Honeycutt College for Women."

Which she had done, and she had lived another twenty-two years in a kind of hermitage on campus and never written another word. From what little she had read and heard, Elise knew young Adela had been extremely successful both as an actor and as a businesswoman. She'd had, in fact, no inherited wealth—she'd come by her money honestly, and from what Elise could gather so far, she'd enjoyed her twin professions immensely. What could have happened to make her so bitter? And why, when she'd left the City, had she also stopped writing and acting? Was her creativity sparked by what she later believed to be the "cynical and jaded" life in San Francisco?

Elise had reason to be interested. First, she was herself an actor, and second, she'd already endured enough of her own empty promises to know she'd go crazy if she didn't make some changes. There *did* have to be something more. She lay her head on her desk and closed her eyes.

9

Chapter Two

Elise Lemoine sat splay-legged in front of the cluttered desk, her hands resting on her thighs, so that she was as close to horizontal as one could get in an uncomfortable, straight-backed wooden chair. Maiju Rittola, tapping a pencil against her temple, seemed otherwise to barely breathe. She had been reading Elise's proposal for five minutes now. Since it was only two pages long, and she had reached the second page quite a while ago, Elise couldn't imagine what she was doing.

Elise attempted to sink further into her chair, the better to escape her confused emotions. Yes, she was annoyed at Professor Rittola, who had greeted her coolly and seemingly without interest. Yes, she would once again complain to the administration about delivering her up to this arrogant new faculty member who appeared not to know that Elise was the toast of Adela Honeycutt College and should be treated with respect. And yes, Maiju Rittola was so desirable that Elise was having trouble accomplishing even the most basic motions of life, like swallowing and breathing.

Exotic was how Frances had described Maiju Rittola. Elise supposed that was a good start, though it only covered the superficial. Professor Rittola had dark, short hair that fluffed around her face in soft curls. Her forehead was narrow, but her face widened at eye-level and then diminished again, almost like the triangular mask of a Siamese cat. Her deep blue eyes had only the barest hint of a fold, the mark of her Lapp heritage. She was dressed exquisitely, in a silk shirt and blousy trousers that demurely accentuated the soft curves of her breasts and hips. In short, she was stunning, and it was all Elise could do not to drown in her.

Professor Rittola raised her head from the page she had been staring at for so long. Her eyes widened with surprise. "Can't you sit up straight?" she chided.

Elise bolted upright, swallowing hard, an unfortunate combination that made her choke for a moment before she recovered her breath. "Ah—" she began, in an effort to explain herself, but Maiju interrupted.

"I find your proposal interesting," she said, fixing Elise with a midnight-blue stare, "but vague."

Elise had managed to stop choking. "Vague," she repeated, her resentment at being made to look foolish darkening her own green eyes. "Well, since I'll be working from primary materials and I haven't started yet, it would be silly to pretend I could be precise." Excellent, she congratulated herself. Then she wondered with sinking heart if she had just accused Maiju Rittola of being silly.

Far from being insulted, however, Maiju was hiding a small smile behind two fingers as she supported her chin on her thumb. "I see. But certainly you have some idea where you're going with this subject."

But certainly, Elise thought with panic. She licked at her dry lips, becoming furious with herself, and, by extension, with Professor Rittola. Why Frances believed it would be pleasurable to be tongue-tied in the presence of this commanding and bewitching woman was more than Elise could fathom. On the other hand, Frances would never imagine that Elise could be so undone. "Of course I have an idea," Elise insisted. "I—"

But Maiju Rittola waved off her explanation, as if, Elise thought angrily, it would be too wearisome to hear.

"How," she asked instead, "did these letters and papers of Adela Honeycutt come to light?"

"Through the great-granddaughter of her friend Sissy Carmichael," Elise explained, glad to be on firmer ground. "It's kind of a funny story, actually. The granddaughter had inherited the house, along with an attic full of junk. She just never went through anything. But last summer a raccoon family got into her attic, and they tore apart some old cartons and scattered papers all over. When the grand-daughter chased out the raccoons and examined the papers, she realized they were Adela Honeycutt's ledgers, diary pages, and letters. So she packed everything up and sent it to the college."

Maiju was actually smiling now. "Where was this raccoon-plagued attic?"

"In New York state, in Rye," Elise said. "The letters—"

But Elise ground to a halt. Her professor had blanched at the mention of Rye; Maiju's shoulders had jerked, as if she'd been slapped, and a mask had slammed down across her face as she tried unsuccessfully to hide the turmoil that welled up in her eyes. Was she frightened? Grief-stricken? Elise couldn't tell, but it was obvious Maiju Rittola was in pain.

"Please continue," Maiju said. Her voice was cold.

Elise nodded, bewildered, and then rushed ahead with her story. "I was just going to say that the letters I've found so far were written by Adela Honeycutt to Sissy Carmichael and to another woman who lived in Sacramento. Really all I've done is to try to order the stuff by date. No one but me's looked at anything since it arrived."

"That seems unlikely." Though Maiju was still remote, she had begun to recover her poise.

"Well, not really," Elise responded. "For one thing, there's an awful lot of material—playbills, receipts, sketches of sets, employee records. They're in three huge cartons. I've only just started on one of them. And also, after you've been here awhile, you'll see that nobody, staff or students, has time for anything extra. It's not the librarian's job to dig through Adela Honeycutt's old papers. And the administration has plenty to do and no money to hire someone else to do it."

Maiju nodded. She was apparently familiar with the excessive commitments of a college administrator—or at least the claims to such.

"You brought some of the letters with you? Read me one."

"All right," Elise said. "Here's when she's just arrived in San Francisco."

❦

14 April, 1856

Dearest Sissy:

At last, San Francisco!

The ship was beautiful, of course, with her tall masts and white sails, like a perfect stage set painted by a master. And the long sea voyage was certainly an adventure! I wished often you and Arthur could have shared the excitement with us, but certainly not the attendant misery. The world is an exotic, amazing, and savage place, the South American ports not very much like New York or Boston. They are dangerous and dark with intrigue and poverty, but yet so colorful, with musicians in the streets and vendors of every imaginable delicacy. Although we were warned not to stray too far on our own at night, I insisted, many times, that we wander deep into the native quarters. And what could Freddy do but go along?

We passed through a terrible storm at the Cape that I was sure would carry us all the way to the South Pole. Freddy was horribly sick. We celebrated my twenty-fifth birthday in our smelly little cabin, he with a dreadful draught from the ship's doctor, I with champagne. We docked yesterday, finally, exhausted but victorious. We are about to discover if what they say is true—that San Francisco is an actor's paradise, the streets literally paved with theaters.

Love always,
Adela

When Elise looked up from her reading, she caught her professor in an unguarded moment: The crisp lines of her jaw and mouth had softened, and her eyes had become faraway and tender. The contrast between the glimpse of inner torment earlier and this mood of serenity was marked. But the moment Maiju realized Elise was staring at her, she came back to herself, all business. "So Adela had quite a turn of phrase. And I hear you too are an actor?"

Where had Maiju run across that bit of information? Of course, it wasn't exactly a state secret—Elise had starred in *A Doll's House* last year—but on the other hand, the news of her triumph had not likely reached New Haven. So how...it was Maiju's turn to be staring curiously, and Elise hurried to answer. "I am. Or I suppose I should say at least I hope to be." She smiled. "In real life, I mean, not just in college. That's part of why..." She hesitated, wondering how much she should reveal to this disturbing woman. In fact, given that she intended to dump her newly appointed advisor as soon as possible, why should she reveal a thing? Yet perhaps because of the turmoil that had washed across her teacher's face, Elise thought Professor Rittola might understand, and that was reason enough to tell her. There was part of herself, she knew, that was terribly lonely, and that part would always try to make a link with someone who could hear her. "You see, I'd like to know why Adela stopped acting. I want to know why she had to retreat from it. What I've heard is that she became disgusted with the shallowness of theater society. Somehow it seems that it must have been more than that. I wondered—oh, I don't know."

"Whether you too will become disgusted?"

Elise floundered for an instant, afraid Maiju was teasing her. But no, she was leaning forward, listening intently. "I'm not asking Adela Honeycutt to predict the future for me, if that's what you mean. But I do want my life to be meaningful, to be deeper."

Maiju pulled back, smiling, and Elise felt a surge of disappointment. She had hoped her professor would understand how important this was to her, but instead

Maiju simply found her entertaining. Elise's disappointment turned to anger as Maiju said in dismissal, "I suppose that's what we all want. And now, Elise—"

"I want my life to be deeper than it has been so far," Elise continued inexorably, determined to get it out now that she'd started. "I'm the only one I have."

They both stared at each other, surprised at their own nakedness in the face of Elise's statement. "You're right," Maiju said. There was an edge of bitterness to her words. Elise was again bewildered. She had been right about one thing: Maiju Rittola was sensitive enough to listen, but that comprehension resulted in walls rather than bridges. What has hurt you so much, Elise wondered. What happened to you? As if sensing Elise's questions, Maiju turned to gaze out the window, cutting off the contact, while Elise quickly gathered together her things.

" 'Til next time, Elise," Maiju said, still facing the big willow tree that guarded one of the levees. She didn't sound very happy about the prospect. Elise walked outside and gazed into the still, gray water in the bottom of the levee. Not very happy? Well, that made two of them.

Chapter Three

Jamie Mahoney was a jock. She stood five-seven in her stocking feet, with well-muscled arms and legs. Her short hair stood up in spikes and she wore a single gold post in the lobe of her left ear. Her blue eyes could bore through you if you gave her a chance, so when Elise, strolling dreamily through fields lining the Sacramento River, heard the familiar whine of Jamie's Yamaha cruising the river road, she scrambled down the bank and stood facing the water, her shoulders hunched, looking as unlike herself as she could. A moment later, the engine quit and running shoe-shod feet came crunching through the withered corn stalks. "Good try, Elise," Jamie said. She was wearing white shorts, and her thighs were tan and bulging with smooth muscles. She flung herself down in the tall grass lining the bank and picked up a pebble and threw it into the river. "You've been avoiding me."

Elise shook her head, though most certainly she had been. She didn't even want to look at Jamie. It was too hard to stay away from her as it was. And it still hurt to see Jamie with her steady procession of cute young things, none of whom really stood a chance with the handsome jock because everyone knew Jamie was interested in only one woman—Elise Lemoine.

"Why, Elise?" Jamie asked. "Why can't we make it work?"

Jamie flipped another rock into the river. It was starting to get chilly. Elise shivered. If she had to see Jamie, this was certainly the last place she would choose, alone, next to this serene, slow river that made everything seem possible...

"Why *would* it work?" Elise asked. "Doesn't it make more sense to ask that? It never has. We're like oil and water, Jamie; there's no point in continuing to try."

Jamie said nothing for a moment. And then, pinning Elise with her sea-colored eyes, she said, "No one can do what I do to you."

God, it was true, that was the terrible part. Elise could already feel the wetness starting, feel her body begin to lean in Jamie's direction as if Jamie had a magnetic field that simply pulled Elise toward her. The river disappeared for a moment, the sighing wind replaced by Jamie mumbling close to her ear. "You want me," Jamie said.

Elise exhaled a breath she felt she'd been holding for months. "Jamie—"

Jamie's lips were against her neck, brushing her skin with silk, her tongue trailing a thin line of fire towards the base of Elise's throat. Something was wrong, but Elise couldn't remember what. When had Jamie risen to her knees? And when had she herself sat down? Jamie's thigh rubbed against her own, and Elise began to melt into her, knowing what Jamie would do now, knowing how it would feel as Jamie grasped Elise's jaw with one firm hand and turned her to face her, reached behind Elise's neck with her other hand and drew her close. Elise's mouth opened hungrily as Jamie's thumb ran hard across her lower lip. A bird called. Called again. The wind rifled Elise's blouse. Jamie moaned against Elise's mouth, removed her thumb only to replace it with her tongue. Elise had the sensation of falling but she didn't seem to go anywhere. Her shoulders hit sand. The bird wailed, wept.

"No!" Elise cried, shoving Jamie off and struggling to her own knees. "Stop it!" She rubbed her hand across her face if only not to see the shock replacing passion in Jamie's eyes.

"Don't do this to us," Jamie pleaded, her voice husky with desire. "You do want me."

"Just because I want you doesn't make it right," Elise said shakily. She slumped down again, her body turned toward the river, away from Jamie. How many times did they have to try to see it was a terrible mistake?

"I don't understand you," Jamie told her.

Elise nodded. "That is so right. You don't. God, I wish you did."

Jamie said nothing, remaining on her knees, her shoulders drooping, the picture of despair. Elise almost reached out to comfort her but didn't dare. It's all an act anyway, Elise told herself. She felt mean and confused and frightened all at once. "I've got to go," she said. She pushed herself out of the sand.

Jamie didn't jump up. She did everything with a slow grace that made women crazy with lust. When Jamie Mahoney rose to her feet, women waited as Elise did now, as if her own feet were stuck to the river bottom. "I'll take you back," Jamie offered.

"No," Elise said. To her fury, it came out a whimper.

"Elise…" Jamie breathed, "don't do this, baby." She brushed her fingertips across Elise's cheekbone.

But Elise twisted away. "No!" she said, her voice now far more certain than the turmoil churning inside warranted. She began storming through the corn, going faster than Jamie would ever walk, flying away from Jamie, feeling like a fool, and with every step she took a little piece of her seemed to die.

Elise escaped to her room. She paced until she was breathing more normally, and then she threw herself down on her bed and pulled out one of Adela's letters from the early years. Anything was better than thinking about Jamie.

🍂

Dearest Sissy:

It's true, it really is—San Francisco is an actor's paradise. New theaters open every day, dozens of plays, operas, extravaganzas of every sort are mounted every year.

Best of all, San Francisco loves her actresses! Here we are not ever treated as a necessary evil, mere adjuncts to the great male stars and still somehow more wicked and disreputable than they. Here, in the Wild West, where the theater itself is respectable (by comparison, I expect, to everything else), women are rare jewels in the roughest of settings, and we actresses are worshiped and idolized far above the actors. Many of the biggest stars are women, and I am determined to be one of them.

I played Puck during the summer! And now Freddy and I have joined the company at Mr. Tom Maguire's brand new Opera House. It is a quite advanced and amazing theater, the first in San Francisco to be lit entirely by gas lamps. He built it after his old theater burned down, a disaster that seems to happen with some regularity here. Freddy says it's because they build them too quickly.

Mr. Maguire is a very clever man, with theaters from here to Virginia City. He is very handsome, too. A shanty Irishman from New York who is also an impresario. They say he can neither read nor write. Freddy thinks our future is certainly with this man, but I am not sure I like him very much. I will learn to adore him, however, if he lets me play Juliet.

You will be astounded to hear, I am sure, that Mr. Maguire's chief rival is a woman named Catherine Sinclair—yes, a woman! A fine actress who also manages a theater. She often starred opposite the great Edwin Booth, before he left to return to the East. Our friends here say the city misses him sorely, and that may be, but there are so many, many, many of us here now who are great or will become great that I think we need not miss anyone who has gone!

All my love,
Adela

Lucky Adela. What would it be like to be faced with such opportunity? Sometimes Elise felt she had grown up in the most stale society imaginable. Adela didn't have to worry that she'd never be able to buy a house or that she had to support herself for umpteen dozens of years and then probably die a lonely pauper anyway. Adela could have lived off Freddy if she hadn't wanted to be a famous actor. Adela had a choice to be famous. So many of us here who will become great, indeed! That's what we're hoping for too, Adela, but the current lot of "so many of us" have what we call diminished expectations, a concept that you, striking out on a new frontier, couldn't even comprehend.

But that wasn't what was really bothering her, Elise admitted. It was Jamie. Or not Jamie so much as her whole love life. When she'd been a kid, twelve, thirteen, she figured she'd marry the first woman she slept with. It'd always been women with her, and there was never going to be more than one—the one. Well, Elise had stopped counting long ago, and now, at the age of twenty, she was sick of it. What good did it do to have a string of women, none of them capable of reaching inside her and touching her heart? It was shallow, stupid, disgusting. And why Jamie wanted to continue being shallow and stupid with her Conquest-of-the-Week was beyond Elise. Maybe if Jamie had come back to school this fall with an entirely new outlook on life, as Elise had, maybe Elise would have tried it again. Maybe. But Jamie hadn't. They'd been back at school only nine days, and Elise had already spotted Jamie squiring around two different women. No, it was Jamie-as-usual, pledging her troth to Elise while diddling a few on the side. Monogamy forever, Elise, the moment you say the word!

I don't want to be tied down, Elise thought. But why? Wasn't that the idea behind the one and only love? Perhaps she only didn't want to be tied down to Jamie. So what about Maiju Rittola? Now where had that ridiculous idea come from? She didn't even know if the professor with the darting midnight eyes was lesbian. Well, not true—she did know, because of the old sixth sense...

And the sixth sense was telling her the professor was lovelorn, too. What else could have caused that anguish in her office when Elise had mentioned Rye? Why Rye? Had Maiju lived there? Did her lover live there? But many things can cause grief, Elise scolded herself. The death of a parent. The death of her dreams. The death of her lover. Now she was back to the lovelorn part. Anyway, she didn't care about Maiju Rittola. The woman was an insensitive lout— well, no, not exactly that, but she certainly wasn't interested in Elise, she'd made that clear enough. And if Elise had a lick of sense, she'd be over at the administration building, trying to get her independent study project switched back to Mr. Danielo. So what if Maiju Rittola were hurting as much as Elise? Was that any reason for Elise to put up with her arrogance and rudeness?

Elise stared moodily out her window. Maiju Rittola would think Elise immature, callow, would probably see no difference between Elise and those asinine freshmen who fluttered around Jamie like moths drawn to the flame. How did one develop the sort of intensity and depth that would attract a woman like Maiju Rittola? For a start, Elise told herself with disgust, by not asking self-serving questions like that. Grow up, girl. Grow the hell up.

Chapter Four

The theater was mobbed with forty-eight wannabe Juliets. Elise shook her head. Why Ralph Goldberg, head of the drama department, had chosen Romeo and Juliet as the fall play was beyond her. There weren't that many great roles for women in it, and Elise believed Ralph had twin responsibilities: good opportunities for his flock of budding actors and challenging plays for his sometimes rough Sacramento Delta audience. In fact, playing the Delta was not unlike Adela's experience:

❦

Sacramento, California
18 July, 1857

Dearest Sissy:

A dreadful, hot summer on the road. I am exhausted, and long to return to the cool beauty of our city by the Bay, although I must say, our overpriced boarding house began to feel a bit cramped last winter, when it rained interminably and I felt I would sink into the mud forever.

No, I am not disillusioned with San Francisco and our life, although Freddy chafes, sometimes,

23

for the easier days in New York. Easier days, indeed! I tell him. Certainly living was cheap enough—you would not believe the prices here. People pay as much as $50.00 for a box seat at the best theaters. But as you well know, I, at least, never seemed to be able to find the roles I wanted. Out here there is so much, that even the hardships are welcome. Although, certainly, we don't always have all the costumes and stage properties that you have in the East.

We have been on the road, now, for two months, and are taking a brief respite from the mining towns, where the accommodations are taxing, to say the least, with lumpy, hard beds, dusty rugless floors, and fighting and shouting all night long. The wildest of the Wild West! The audiences are wonderful, though, only a bit rougher and rowdier than those in San Francisco, and so many of the miners are educated men—former doctors and lawyers brush elbows here with the most questionable people! They all come hungry for the Bard and if one of us forgets her lines, the audience is ready with them!

A week ago I saw a gunfight and a man died. They were fighting over a prostitute. Not to say that kind of thing never happens in San Francisco, of course—I've simply never been standing on the same street at the same time before! In San Francisco, some of our leading citizens—Mr. Tom Maguire himself, for an example—have been known to brawl or even duel at the slightest provocation.

It's all very exciting. Some actors tire of it and return East. So many (and why not my dearest friends, then?) visit from time to time as stars from the East. But I find it all to my liking and feel that this is where my life and future lie. My dear husband is not so sure as I, I am afraid, and speaks wistfully sometimes of New York.

I suppose you two still insist on staying there? And Arthur is doing well? I am glad he is doing well, but wish you could be here, where the true excitement and fun are. I miss you terribly, Sissy. I have no one so close to me here.

The temperature passed one hundred degrees in this capital city last night. We were invited to a soiree at the home of a local theater patron and met many lovely people, sweltering and perspiring and maintaining their composure through it all.

Among those we met was a charming young girl named Sylvia Woodruff, a child of seventeen so fascinated by the theater and by our lives that she quite surrounded me with her attention most of the evening. She talked of her own love for Shakespeare and for the theater.

The young Sylvia also talked of college in the East—college! She says there actually is one for young women, in Milwaukee, I believe she said. And those Beecher women—you know of the writer, Harriet—are somehow involved in it. Sylvia says the school is very new and is much superior to the women's seminaries and normal schools. How sweet to be so youthful, with a world open to you and all your choices in the future! She is the dearest and most adorable of young women. We became great friends and she pressed me to promise that we would correspond.

So you see, now you must come West, or I shall have too many letters to write!

Love always,
Adela

Of course, Sissy and Arthur had not come West, according to Sissy's great-granddaughter, and for some reason the letters Adela had written to the young Sylvia had also ended up in Sissy's possession. From Elise's initial sorting by date (she was a third of the way through the second carton by now), more than half the letters appeared to be addressed to Sylvie.

"Woolgathering?" Ralph Goldberg threw himself down in the chair next to Elise so hard the entire connected row of seats jounced like a carnival ride. He grinned at her. Thirty-two, with curly blond-brown hair and funny crooked teeth that were too big for his mouth, he was adorable, a Puck of a man. If I were straight, Elise thought...but of course that was ridiculous.

"What'd you do all summer?" He raised his eyebrows, preparing to be entertained. He had once interceded in a fight between her and Jamie late in her freshman year, when she'd been a know-nothing in his big Introductory Theater class. Before then she would have been hard-pressed to prove that he'd ever noticed her, but when he saw the two women arguing outside the stage entrance to the theater, he was at Elise's side in an instant, catching her elbow and carrying her away from a furious Jamie as he jabbered about some stage props she was supposed to find. She was so fooled by his obliviousness that her mouth dropped open when he swung her around to make certain Jamie had stalked off and said, "Maybe you should pick someone who doesn't have quite as mean a left hook as that one probably does." When she'd tried to dredge up a response, he'd shaken his head and said, "I mean it, Elise. You're someone special. Start taking yourself seriously." Then he'd smiled at her and left her standing bemused in front of a bed of fiery red tulips. He'd never mentioned the incident afterward, but several times he'd told her that she would have to be careful in her public life, and once he'd even begun a sentence with, "A woman of your proclivities..."

"This summer?" She thought about his question. "Nothing of interest," she told him. She smiled at his eager face. He was such a kind man. "I've decided to follow your advice and take myself seriously."

"That's very good. Does that mean Left-Hook is gone?"

She was amazed he even remembered. "Just about," she admitted.

He grinned at her, and then turned his attention to the stage. "Now which of these young ladies do you think should be Juliet?"

"I—ah..." Since Elise planned to audition for the part herself, this was a loaded question. But she loved to speculate with him, loved the easy give-and-take which had developed between them last year. She had, in fact, become Ralph's right hand, his production assistant as well as one of his star performers. "Me, of course. That aside, I suspect Linda Martinez would be good. She's got that ingenue look. Or Pam Brandi, same reason."

"Tina Freeman?" he asked. He nodded at Tina across the room. She had long, straight hair and a pale face, and she moved like a dancer. Elise had seen her with Jamie just the other day.

"She's a freshman," Elise said. It was an unspoken rule that freshmen didn't get starring parts. "Also she seems a little affected." She walks around on the tips of her toes, for heaven's sake, Elise grumbled to herself. What was Ralph thinking of?

Ralph was nodding, watching his charges, catching the byplay between his male graduate students and the younger women. Supposedly he put the fear of god into his male students every September. He promised them that if they screwed around with the freshmen, he'd put their pricks in a sling... And no one did, mostly because a phone call from Ralph Goldberg to a theater company in the City could launch a career.

"I've been thinking of Strindberg or Chekhov in the spring," he told Elise. "In fact, I'm considering doing three major plays this year, one in February, one in May, plus all the readings and workshops." He smiled at her. "So nothing happened all summer?"

"Nothing," she affirmed.

"Well, I'm glad you rested up because plenty will be happening here."

Later, as she walked back to her dorm, she wished she could believe him.

Chapter Five

Elise docked her late-model Mustang—the only visible residue of her modeling career—under a bedraggled willow tree and slid off the cool leather upholstery into the dripping Delta heat. There were two ways to get to Lulu's Bar & Restaurant: a quick walk across the footbridge from Honeycutt Island or a fifteen-minute roundabout drive to the far side of the island, across the drawbridge to the mainland, and then back to the bar. Elise had chosen to enjoy the Mustang's frigid air conditioning, but now she was twice as hot as before. She was suddenly exhausted and not at all sure why she'd made the trip in the first place.

The bar was open as long as possible under California law, from six a.m. to two a.m., and it had customers every minute of that twenty hours. The patrons were a weird amalgam of wealthy Honeycutt students, crusty fishermen and farmers, the usual assortment of alkies who became more sodden year by year, and a few tourists from San Francisco or beyond who wandered in to blink confusedly at the mix. Lulu himself, beer-bellied and bald-headed, served beer and greasy hamburgers with a grunt, and kept an eagle eye on the Honeycutt girls to make certain they weren't annoying the rest of his sterling clientele.

He grinned now at Elise. "Junior," he said. Lulu had a counter in his head that told him when a Honeycutt girl had attained her junior year, which to him signified legal drinking age even if it didn't to the state of California. The cops had apparently decided to go along with Lulu's system, since he'd never been busted for selling beer to twenty-year-olds.

"Draft," Elise said. "Have a nice summer, Lulu?"

He shrugged. "Tourists," he said. "Houseboaters. Assholes." By local legend, Lulu had gotten his name when he was with the occupation forces in Germany during the early '50s. How anyone had gotten close enough to give him a nickname was beyond Elise's imagination. And why "Lulu," she'd never been able to learn.

She sipped her beer and stared into the gloom. Lulu's was the darkest bar she'd ever been in. Some said it was so the women from the college wouldn't have to see the locals, but Elise was certain it was the other way around. Lulu liked his college clientele, but Honeycutt students were not popular with the rest of the townspeople. Too rich, too young, too cute, too stuck-up. The "toos" went on and on. Jealousy, Elise thought, or simply that we're different. People don't like another tribe living on their doorstep, and that's definitely what the Honeycutt crowd was.

Good old Adela. If only she'd considered the weather before she set up her women's college. Perhaps if she'd opted for the Sierra...

❧

27 September, 1857

My Dear Sylvie:

I am delighted to hear that your parents are bringing you to San Francisco for your eighteenth birthday in November. Best news of all, you will be able to see me as Hamlet at the Metropolitan! Catherine Sinclair says I am the finest Hamlet she ever saw, including, she said, Edwin Booth.

I remember we talked, at your house in Sacramento, about the wonderful roles women are asked to play in San Francisco. And now I am to join that great company of leading ladies who have played Hamlet—I have even heard that the famous international adventuress, the beautiful and wicked Lola Montez—have you heard of her, in Sacramento?—tried the role a few years ago, but gave it up quickly and returned to her amazing Spider Dance after all. Probably for the best.

I would like also to play both Lady Macbeth and Macbeth himself—although not at the same time!

Your dear, kind words of encouragement and affection mean so much to me... I cannot wait to perform for you and hear you say how wonderful I am!

And you, my darling young friend? What will you do? Will you go away to college and become a great intellectual? I think you will. And leave your friends behind to pine away.

> Eagerly awaiting your visit, I remain
> Your friend,
> Adela

Elise sighed, folded up the photocopied letter, and signaled for another beer. Reading in this dungeon was next to impossible and besides, she was getting too wrapped up in Adela's life, though it was a welcome relief from the doldrums of her own existence. But surely disappearing into the past wasn't healthy. She needed to make an effort to meet people. Adela was a good example. She'd evidently found a friend in Sylvie.

After Lulu had plunked the beer down in front of her, spilling half the head on the tacky surface of the bar, Elise swiveled around on her stool to watch the pool game that was always going on at the back of the room. But as her eyes roamed past the red booths toward the rear, she stopped and did a double take. That person sitting by herself, huddled over a drink, looked like—Elise could scarcely see through the darkness—Maiju Rittola. What on

31

earth would *she* be doing here? But it was Professor Rittola, of that Elise was certain. Faculty members did come to Lulu's on occasion, but they normally escaped the Delta entirely or drank on campus, at the pub. Maiju wouldn't know that, of course, and what difference did it make anyway? Elise stood up before she really knew what she was doing and made her way over to Maiju's booth.

"Hi!" Elise said brightly, her beer cradled at her side.

Maiju started, and for a moment her eyes were unguarded. She looks wary, Elise thought with a shock, like a fox on the run. Could she find me frightening? Then she realized she was gaping at her professor. She closed her mouth with an effort and took a deep breath, wishing she had just flung herself onto the bench opposite Maiju when she'd arrived. The time had passed for spontaneity; now she would have to wait for an invitation to sit.

Meanwhile the mask of reserve had snapped tight over Maiju's face. "Well, hello, Elise," she said coolly. "I didn't know they allowed students in here."

I'm supposed to be here, not you, Elise wanted to say, but she remained silent. She raised her glass of beer and sipped at it, mesmerized by the clear deep blue of Maiju's eyes gleaming in the flat dark of the bar. The hollow click of balls careening into each other on the pool table punctuated a low wailing song on the jukebox. The two women watched each other, the wariness slipping back into Maiju's face, echoed now by Elise's own. Suddenly Elise knew that they were both trying to hide the evidence of that caution because it stemmed from desire.

Elise sipped again at her beer. Maiju did not motion for her to sit down. Instead she said, "I understand you've been trying to switch your independent study project back to Mr. Danielo."

"That was before I met you," Elise blurted and then cursed herself. Jesus, talk about a come-on! Maiju's face looked frozen. "I mean," Elise hurried on, "after I talked to you about my proposal, I felt fine about it." A lie. Each day she intended to trek over to the administration building,

32

but she never managed to make it there. It would be a lie to say she felt fine about Maiju Rittola as well.

Maiju recovered her equilibrium and appeared startled to see Elise still standing in front of her. "Well," she began, "perhaps you should sit—"

"Hey, Elise!" Jamie's slow voice came from just behind her. Elise couldn't believe it—just when Maiju had finally asked her to join her. Elise turned for help to Maiju, hoping she would deliver a few well-chosen words that would send Jamie slinking away. But instead Elise was seared by the palpable relief spreading across Maiju's face. Elise's free hand tightened into a fist, her nails digging into the palm.

"C'mon, babe, sit with us," Jamie said, patting Elise's behind in what could have been a comradely gesture, but which Elise knew was meant to signal possession to whomever Elise was talking. And that someone got the message. Maiju glanced down at her drink with a faint smile, accepting Jamie's claim, even as Elise gritted her teeth in anger.

"Well, hi," Jamie drawled to Maiju, as if she'd just noticed Elise wasn't talking to an empty booth. "I'm Jamie Mahoney. I don't believe…" She let her voice trail away as she stuck out her hand, a broad grin on her face, magnanimous now that she'd won. Damn your sureness, Jamie, Elise thought, damn you!

"Maiju Rittola," Maiju responded, touching Jamie's hand briefly, and then stretching. "It's getting rather late, isn't it?"

"Not hardly," Jamie said. "Would you care to join us?"

"Oh, I don't believe so," Maiju said. "I have to be getting back. Good night, Elise."

It was a dismissal. There was no other way of interpreting it. Elise nodded and turned away, turned away with full-of-herself Jamie, whom Elise wanted to strangle. "Little old for you, isn't she?" Jamie winked on the way over to her crowd of soccer buddies. Elise didn't answer. She refilled her beer glass from their pitcher and crunched into a corner, ignoring Jamie's efforts to draw her into the conversation. When Elise finally looked again toward the rear of the bar, Maiju's booth was empty.

Chapter Six

"So what about Jamie?" Frances asked. She had gobbled up nearly the entire plate of french fries in the three minutes since the waitress had set them on the table.

"Haven't you eaten lately?" Elise asked.

Frances grinned around another fry. "No time. The married one? His wife has a perpetual headache."

Elise snorted. "Where's it going to get you, Frances? I mean, ultimately."

"Ul-ti-mate-ly..." Frances dragged out the syllables, "it's going to get me in-ti-ma-cy. As in 'get laid,' baby."

"I'm sure it's getting you that already," Elise said disapprovingly.

Frances stopped eating long enough to stare at her roommate. "Boy, that first week I thought you were on the rag or something, Elise, but now it's been going on too long. What's the deal here? I liked it better when you were sobbing over Jamie every night."

"Thanks. And I never was sobbing over Jamie."

"Oh, really. Okay." Frances was down to nibbling now. Elise picked at her chef's salad. She wished she'd gotten the Greek. She should have known they'd use dyed orange cheese and processed ham at this disgusting diner. What could they manage to wreck in a Greek salad?

"Elise, do you want me to talk to Jamie for you?"

Elise threw down her hard roll in a fury. "Why do you keep plugging Jamie? Has she paid you a fee? I mean, my god…"

"It's just that you've gone together for such a long time—"

"We've never really gone together at all—"

"Oh, that's unfair, Elise."

It was, but Elise had a point too, and Frances knew it. Jamie and Elise's relationship had been tumultuous from the beginning, when Jamie had blithely slept around on Elise, apparently believing that while Elise would toe the fidelity line, she was free to play. "But it doesn't mean anything!" she had howled at Elise when Elise confronted her.

"Fine, then I guess I don't either," Elise said. She had been deeply hurt. Jamie had been only her second relationship, after a disturbing three-year-long high school romance with Ruth, who burst into guilty sobs every time they made love. Elise had stuck it out with Ruth long past the point of sense itself, partially because of her longing to commit herself to her first lover, and also because she had honestly believed she could eventually help Ruth accept her lesbianism. On that front, Jamie had been a welcome relief—for Jamie, being a lesbian was cause for celebration —but she brought other baggage with her to the relationship, such as her adherence to a double standard Elise found incomprehensible.

Elise, smarting and determined to pay Jamie back, had begun her now legendary conquest of the freshman class, a goal which Jamie quickly adopted as her own. The two remained in competition throughout the latter semester of their freshman year, occasionally sleeping with each other as a relief from the hunt. During each of these respites, Jamie begged Elise to settle down with her, claiming that she had been a fool in those early days, and that she would swear fidelity and whatever else Elise could think of to demand.

Jamie had even taken a sublet in Oakland for the summer, arriving twice weekly in the City to hang around Elise's doorstep until Elise's parents relented and let her in the house. Elise herself finally gave in toward the end of August, believing that if Jamie loved her this much it had to work. And it did, for about six blissful weeks. But once the big prize had been bagged and hung on the wall—Elise's angry words to Jamie a few months later—Jamie was content to let things rest. When they returned to school, Jamie spent nearly every evening hanging out with her jock pals. She never showed the slightest interest in anything Elise was doing, in spite of the fact that during Elise's sophomore year she made an enormous splash in the drama department. Elise, in fact, had to beg Jamie to come see *A Doll's House*—and the parallels between her life and the play simply became too much. Elise dumped her the next week, and as far as Jamie was concerned, the hunt was on again. This time Elise was determined not to give in, although her body betrayed her at the most annoying times, leaping to attention whenever Jamie sauntered by. All Elise could do was avoid Jamie as much as possible.

"Do you really want me to be miserable?" Elise asked Frances. "'Cause that's what I'd be with Jamie."

"She's very attractive," Frances said.

"Yes, she is. She's charming, funny, cute, and a bunch of other lovely things. She's also a total egoist and a jerk, and she's in love with Jamie being in love with Elise, she's not in love with Elise. There's your answer, Frances. I'm not going to put up with it. I'm going to take myself seriously this year. I should have done it a long time ago."

Frances sighed. "I can see it's going to be a grim winter. You and your Adela Honeycutt project. How are you getting along with Ms. Gorgeous Maiju Rittola?"

"Fine."

Frances ate around the edges of her hamburger. This habit of hers, nibbling around burgers as if they were ears of corn, drove Elise wild. "Take a real bite, Frances, for god's sake!"

"I wonder why you don't say more about her." Frances watched Elise speculatively. "Have you figured out if she's a dyke yet?"

Frances was the only straight person Elise knew who could use the "d" word and sound halfway natural about it. "She's a dyke," Elise confirmed.

"Sure?"

"Absolutely."

Frances stared at her over her hamburger, which had diminished to a silver-dollar-sized center. "How can you be so certain? I mean, I don't understand how this sixth sense operates."

"Never mind, Frances. It's all a myth anyway."

"But then why does it work if it's a myth?"

"Never mind! Listen, if you were going to the school sherry party, what would you wear? If you were me, that is, not you."

Frances made a ghastly face. "The school sherry—ah, you mean if I were you and I was trying to impress Professor Rittola who has to show up at the school sherry party because she's a new faculty member and it would look very uncool if she didn't and since it's the biggest snore this side of Kansas you and Rittola and the dean and the president will probably be the only people there. You mean what would I wear in that case?"

"Exactly," Elise said, drumming her fingers on the red-flecked Formica.

"All right, but let me say this first. I don't approve of this Maiju person. She's a professor, you're a student."

"He's married, you're not," Elise rejoined.

"And she's too old for you. She's gotta be twenty-nine at least. Plus there's something weird about her. And just yesterday you told me she wasn't interested."

"I'm not interested in her either."

"Right. Look, Elise, the last thing you need is more intrigue in your life."

"I think this is a case of the pot and the kettle, Frances. Your intrigue tolerance is about forty times a normal person's. What about my jade sweater?"

"That'd be fine if it weren't a hundred degrees out. How about a French bikini? In fact, go topless. That oughta catch her attention."

"Are you planning to eat that?" Elise asked. She was pointing at the little chunk of hamburger left on Frances's plate. It was perfectly round, the exact center of the burger.

"No, because then I can pretend this was a diet day," Frances said with a grin. "Why, do you want it?"

"I don't intend to eat it. My plan is to grind it in your face—mustard and mayonnaise and wilted lettuce and slimy tomato." She reached for the morsel but Frances caught her wrist.

"I'll help you dress. And I won't say another word, okay? But you have to promise to let me tell you about Don."

"Don's the one with the headachy wife? Maybe she knows something you don't."

Frances plunked thirteen dollars on the table and waved off Elise's attempt to pay. Elise didn't try very hard because Frances always picked up the tab. The recipient of a cool seventy thou per year from a trust fund, Frances spread her money around in discreet ways, like taking Elise to lunch and stocking the dorm refrigerator every few days with beer and munchies. Elise, in turn, kept Frances's secret. There were plenty of wealthy women at Adela Honeycutt, but Frances won the prize for being the most modest. Elise doubted that anybody had a clue the biggest run-around on campus was also one of the richest.

"Turn on the chill," Frances commanded as she hopped in Elise's Mustang. Elise flicked on the stereo as well, and came close to flooring it as they rocketed along the levees. A few farmers shook their heads as they passed, the speeding car trailing snatches of song and laughter.

Chapter Seven

Elise meandered around her room in her mustard yellow Chinese silk robe with the enormous embroidered tiger on the back, humming to herself. She had showered and hung out the dress she and Frances had chosen, a loosely clinging, calf-length garment in a soft aquamarine that made Elise's darker green eyes seem to start from her face. Elise thought it telegraphed an unstudied sensuality perfect for the sherry party. "She'll come running," Frances had concluded after Elise had pulled it on and with a flip of her head tossed her blunt blond mane out of her eyes.

Elise clicked her tongue. "You are incorrigible."

"Simply realistic. Why pretend you're not dressing for her when you are? And why pretend you're dressing for her for any other reason than to get her in bed?"

"Perhaps I'm not," Elise said. She herself couldn't explain why she had woken up this morning so determined to go to the sherry party. Certainly Maiju Rittola had shown no inclination to be receptive to Elise's charms. And why should Elise pursue someone who not only seemed uninterested but actually forbidding? Maybe she was getting as bad as Jamie, chasing whatever eluded her. But she couldn't shake the feeling that behind Maiju's cold exterior was a passionate, sensitive woman struggling to be released... My god, Elise thought suddenly, was this her first lover Ruth all over again? Hadn't she had enough of the savior role?

All this was too depressing. Perhaps she was only trying to inject some drama into a life in which precious little was happening. What she should be doing was studying, not racing off to sherry parties on muddled missions of rescue and seduction. Her Italian class, for instance, was taking a back seat to the Adela Honeycutt project, and she had not read even one play for Mr. Grittell's modern drama course. Grittell had a reputation for being a slave driver, with papers due every two weeks. She should never have chosen such a complex independent study course. She had finally reached the third carton of the Honeycutt material, and thankfully it mostly seemed to be full of ledgers. But wading through all the letters and diaries she'd extracted from the first two cartons was going to be a real chore.

❦

10 November, 1857

Dearest Sissy:

Freddy had an argument with Tom Maguire and abandoned his rehearsals for the lead role in Anna Mowatt's play, *Armand, or The Peer and The Peasant*. He has marched off to the music halls— our best, of course, the Bella Union—to join the cast of their latest minstrel show. He says he will be a comedian and will burlesque every play Maguire does.

Well, I told him, that is all right if you must. I suppose the Bella Union's leg shows are not much different from our own, although they do show more leg—and many more legs. But his endless discontent is beginning to affect me. I am worried for our marriage. We do not seem to understand each other anymore or to agree about anything. I can only wonder, now, if the lack has always existed but has been concealed by the comforts and friendships of New York. I am distraught, and yet…well, sulkiness is tiresome and my very own independent life goes so well.

I am very happy at the Metropolitan this season —have I told you I am doing Hamlet for several weeks? The Melancholy Dane, in doublet and tights, speaking of legs, and of course everyone does.

Delighted to hear you did Desdemona to Edwin Booth's Othello—his friends here are always eager for news of him. And Arthur is producing now? What successes you both are!

I do wish you could see me as Hamlet.

Love always,
Adela

❦

15 December, 1857

Dearest Sylvie:

It was wonderful seeing you again, my dear sweet friend, and Freddy and I so much enjoyed having dinner with you and your charming parents.

No, I did not particularly notice that your father was somehow uncomfortable with me. Perhaps you merely imagined it? Perhaps, in your devotion, you expect everyone else to adore me instantly—I would have thought Freddy an idiot if he had not agreed that you are the most beautiful and delightful young woman in all of California. I think he is quite jealous of our affection. Your mother, by the way, is very lovely. Freddy was also much taken by her, as was I—I think you bear her a striking resemblance.

I'm glad you liked my performance as the Dane. Our notices in the other papers were as good as the one you saw in the *Daily Dramatic Chronicle*.

You are much too modest when you say that you could never be an actress. Perhaps you are too shy, but you would be stunning if you chose our calling. Absolutely stunning. I think the passion you would stir in your audiences would be a cure for the most tenacious shyness.

But I don't wish to influence you—perhaps you should be a female Shakespearean scholar, a famous professor. Or perhaps you will write plays—that would be wonderful for me, to star in a play you wrote. If Mowatt can do it, so can you! I would be most pleased to take direction from such a lovely playwright.

My deepest affection,
Adela

Elise stared at the pages, wondering what the problem was with Sylvie's father. Was he worried that his daughter would adopt the ways of liberated Victorian womanhood and dash off to seek her own fortune? But in that case, why pursue a relationship with the Honeycutts at all? It was so odd to peer at these people from a distance of more than a hundred and thirty years and wonder at their motivations and intentions.

And how incredible that Adela would play Hamlet! We're so much more constrained now, Elise thought, while we believe ourselves to be totally free. She could not imagine a society that spent more energy deluding itself, although from her mother's stories of the '50s, that era took a close second to this one. But maybe in her mother's day, the American Dream was still alive and kicking, for most people at least. What she should do in her effort to take herself seriously was go on one of those Take Back the Night marches or lend her support to the campus pro-choice group instead of distracting herself with sherry parties.

Speaking of which, it was already five-fifteen. She'd meant to arrive right on time, predicting that Maiju would make no more than a quick appearance. She pulled on her dress, ran a brush through her hair, rubbed her fingers across her cheeks to bring up some color—though the brisk walk across campus would take care of that—and dashed out the door. No Frances to see her off; she had already disappeared on a quick spin to the river with Don, who sounded like he knew a good thing when he found it.

As she walked to the party, she found herself worrying about her conversation with Ralph Goldberg. Had he been trying to let her down gently about Juliet? She *had* played Nora in *A Doll's House,* so it was perhaps rather selfish to angle for Juliet as well. But the class above hers, seniors this year, had no real dramatic star material and was filled, instead, with very funny stand-up comics and character actors. Ralph, in fact, had had to adapt his schedule to accommodate them, producing many more intimate "club dates" in the pub, to the delight of their Delta audience. In fact, the senior class had done more to upgrade the image of the college in the eyes of the townies than any group since '86, when nearly the whole school turned out to woman the sandbags during one of the periodic Delta floods, saving acres of valuable farmland.

But now she had come within sight of the sherry party, and as Frances had predicted, it was lightly attended. No more than fifty people wandered between the two long portable tables that held bottles of sherry and ugly plastic glasses and an assortment of hors d'oeuvres that might have been good if they hadn't been made hours ago by the lunch crew. A tall bay tree provided shade and a lovely scent, while randomly set candles were supposed to discourage insects. It all seemed very Southern, Elise thought as she wiped her brow.

So far no sign of the lovely Professor Rittola. Dean Bankston, however, a nasty closet case (so closeted she was married to a man), was bearing down on Elise, her short, wispy hair standing on end from the humidity. "My, my, I don't believe we've ever been graced with your presence at the Welcome party."

Elise smiled sweetly. "Perhaps not," she said, implying that it was certainly not worth remembering or remarking upon.

Mrs. Bankston smiled too, though hers had an ugly feral touch, as if she'd scented a mouse. "Looking for someone?"

"Not really," Elise said languidly. "Perhaps Ralph Goldberg will come."

"I doubt it." Hostility radiated from her eyes. She despised the out lesbians, and had, in fact, called in some of the more obvious women and told them to dress and behave more discreetly. She had caught on too late to Jamie and Elise's semester of freshman-class pillaging, mostly because no one complained—the straight women finding it a fun experiment, and the lesbians glad to be brought out. Besides, Jamie and Elise were both popular, and most everyone saw the sleeping around as an adjunct to their rocky relationship. Since no one had any expectations, no one had gotten too hurt, though now that they'd officially broken up as far as the college grapevine was concerned, Jamie was undoubtedly running roughshod over people's feelings.

"Will you be in any plays this year?"

Of course I will, you old bag, Elise thought, and you know it too. "Probably," she said.

"Anything in particular?"

"Strindberg."

The feral smile became broader. "Ah, Strindberg. I don't really care for him. Too cerebral."

Elise plucked a glass of sherry from the nearby table and sipped it before answering. "That's odd. I find him quite the opposite. He's very intuitive and spiritual."

Mrs. Bankston chuckled. "I see you've learned the most important lesson taught at Adela Honeycutt: how to engage in useless but clever repartee at cocktail parties."

Elise was momentarily floored, not at the sentiment, which was often enough expressed in the dorms, but that the dean herself would say it. And Mrs. Bankston, knowing the effect her statement would produce on Elise, was beginning to smile triumphantly. Help, however, came from an unexpected quarter.

"I should hope that we aspire to teach them a great deal more than that, Mrs. Bankston," said Maiju Rittola, striding up on Elise's left shoulder. Elise whirled to face her and was again stopped short: Maiju was truly magnificent,

46

wearing a pale pink silk blouse and dove gray trousers that billowed lightly around her long, graceful legs. At her throat she had tied a short scarf in blues and the same dawn pink, highlighting the length of her neck. She stood slightly behind Elise, and though she said not another word, Elise felt absolutely protected, as if the ground which had shifted underneath her at the dean's words was now more solid than it had ever been before.

"I'm sure I was joking, Ms. Rittola," Mrs. Bankston said sharply, but in the face of such a strong defense, she turned away to seek easier prey.

"Thank you," Elise said. "I was really taken aback."

"Yes, I could see that you were. She's a very unpleasant person, isn't she?"

"I think that sums it up. Would you care for some sherry?"

"Is it as horrid as it looks?"

"It won't kill you, though it might taste that way." Elise handed Maiju a glass of the amber-colored liquid, which was purchased in bulk from a local winery. Maiju took a sip and suppressed a shudder.

"I'm glad to hear it's not lethal." She smiled at Elise, and Elise's heart began romping. How had she even considered for one second *not* coming to the sherry party? They gazed at each other for a moment, until Maiju turned quickly away. "So," she said, staring up at the overhanging branches of the bay tree, "how is your Adela project going?"

"Just fine," Elise said, disappointed. Back to business. Of course, what had she expected? Maiju certainly would not sweep her off her feet at the Welcome party. No, making a more positive contact was as much as she could hope for. "There's something that keeps bothering me, though," she continued. "I don't understand how Sissy Carmichael ended up with the letters that were sent to the woman in Sacramento."

Maiju stared at the tree so long that Elise began to think she hadn't heard. But finally she looked back at Elise, and the disturbance that had been in her eyes when Elise had mentioned Rye was back. "I imagine there could be many reasons," Maiju said, though she clearly didn't want to speculate on them—in fact, she wanted the subject closed as soon as possible.

"I'm sure you're right," Elise muttered and quickly began talking about the comedy prowess of the senior class. But as she explained the familiar story to Maiju, she was churning inside. Something terrible had happened to Maiju, she thought, something really awful, and Adela Honeycutt somehow reminds her of it. How clever, Elise, to choose a topic that distresses this beautiful woman so much she can hardly bear to look at you.

Chapter Eight

"So she rescued you from Dean Bankston like a knight in shining armor, huh?" Frances was lying in bed, sipping a cappuccino Elise had bought for her at the cafe.

"I wouldn't quite put it that way," Elise said, stretching out across the double bulge of Frances's feet. "But she certainly did stand up for me. It's funny." Elise had been trying to explain her puzzlement to herself since the sherry party thirty-six hours earlier. "I felt so protected, as if I'd never known what that meant before. She was by my side, like a solid rock that I could completely depend on—"

"Except then she wasn't," Frances pointed out.

Elise sighed. "Yes, then she wasn't. Then she was back to Adela Honeycutt and how was my project."

"Could it be you're…fantasizing a bit? Seeing what you want to see? If you were in truth less attached to Jamie, don't you think you'd choose someone more realistic? Someone accessible?"

Elise shook her head. "You don't get it, Frances. Jamie is gone, gone, gone."

"She may be gone from your head, but she hasn't pulled up her claim from your bod, babe. I see how you tense up when she comes by. Especially when she's with Tina Freeman or any of that cute crowd."

"Tina Freeman's a pretentious nerd."

"Precisely," Frances said with a grin. "Anyway, my point is, perhaps it's safer for you now to engage in a bit of harmless romanticizing than to get into something real. And that's probably fine."

Elise unexpectedly burst into tears.

"Oh, Elise! I didn't mean to make you cry." Frances put down her coffee and scooted out from under the covers so she could hold Elise. Rocking her gently, she murmured, "I could just kill Jamie. I'd like to—"

"Frances, do me a favor," Elise said thickly. "Don't mention her name for at least two weeks, okay?"

"Oh, I'm sorry, honey. I'm so dense... But this Maiju—"

"But it was so nice, Frances! I've never felt that way before, that someone really would stand by me like that."

"There'll be others," Frances predicted.

"How do you know?" Elise wailed. "Don't you think that who you should be with is written down in the sky somewhere in a big book, and you have to look through the whole world to find that person but then how can you be sure it's really her because no one can see the book?"

"Jeez, talk about romantic, Elise! No, I don't think that!" She paused, trying to peer at Elise's face. "You don't really believe that dreck, do you?"

"Well, no, but...a little bit, I guess. I mean, don't you, just a little?"

"Of course not. I can't imagine *ever* believing that."

"Don't be patronizing."

"I'm trying not to be, but we're not ten anymore, playing with Ken and Barbie. Or Barbie and Barbie in your case."

Elise heaved a huge sigh. "Oh, Frances, what am I going to do?"

"You don't *need* to do anything. No one's demanding you find Ms. Right today or even next year. So how about going and getting me another cappuccino in the meantime? This one's gotten cold."

"Forget it."

"Ungrateful wench."

"Shameless hussy."

Elise retired to her own room to study. Italian had become tiresome lately, as she was in her second year and it was getting complicated. If only she'd taken Spanish instead of French in high school... And Mr. Grittell's reputation as a taskmaster was proving out. She had signed up for his modern drama literature course, figuring it'd be easy as pie. Grittell, unfortunately, really did demand a paper every two weeks, and no excuses were allowed. This was quite unusual at Adela Honeycutt where PMS, nervous breakdowns, and suicide attempts could be dragged out at appropriate intervals to explain why promised work was delayed. Elise stared at the book of Pirandello plays and decided she couldn't deal with endless encirclements this morning. She had too many of her own. Leafing through Adela's letters was becoming her favorite habitual distraction.

❧

3 June, 1858

My Dear Sissy:

Lady Macbeth!—you have beaten me to the role by only a few months. Bless you—you will be wonderful, as will I!

Freddy's distress grows. He has flung himself back and forth between the Bella Union and the Metropolitan this year, unsettled and unsettling in his ambitions. He had a duel in May and barely came away with his life—pistols in Portsmouth Square. He will not tell me what he was fighting over and I must suspect it was over something, or someone, I'd rather not know about. He has never shown interest in other women before, but for months now I have felt that he was changing. Or I have changed and he finds it insupportable. He has also been drinking too much and is getting thoroughly tiresome. I don't think either of us can bear it much longer.

I am doing Juliet and the famous Mrs. Judah is of course doing her role as the nurse. She is quite a wonderful actress and a kind soul. So tragic, too. To lose one's husband and children in a shipwreck—to watch them slip away—and then to go on as she has. What great courage women have, courage we rarely are credited with.

Lovingly,
Adela

❦

7 December, 1858

Dearest Sylvie:

What! You are not going on to college but are getting engaged? And will be married in June? Well, this is a surprise. Not at all what I thought you wanted for your life, from our conversations here in the fall. But it is what your parents wanted, I see that. Of course it would be. I'm sure you will be very happy, and I want only the greatest happiness for you. Forgive me if I seem jealous of your time and affection—but I am!

Do you love him? Do you love him half as much as I love you, sweet child? Do you love him as much as you love me? Will he be jealous of you and of your affections?

But I must have faith that nothing will come between us in our tender friendship. May I have that faith?

Will I have the pleasure and privilege of meeting this young man anytime soon? Will you be coming to San Francisco? As you see, I am full of questions and you must tell me more.

I will be in Sacramento this spring and you can reassure me then, with an embrace and a gentle kiss, that your heart is still mine. Then I will attend the wedding and throw heaps of rice on

52

you both. And now I shall not say another word on the subject until I see you, except to beg that you not break my heart.

The play I will be doing in Sacramento is a new one, a melodrama. My role is that of a maiden aunt. It's called *The Young Man's Fancy*, and it's rather entertaining, I think.

So I will see you then!

Love,
Adela

❦

17 March, 1859

Dear, Dear Sissy:

Let me be the first to announce the return to the New York theater of the famous Mr. Frederick Honeycutt. I am staying here. Do take him out for a drink or something.

He was actually doing rather well, I thought. He was on the bill with that child darling of the music halls, Lotta Crabtree, and they were pulling in enormous crowds. But he said they were, after all, her crowds, not his.

I'm afraid the truth is, his comedy was not very funny and was becoming increasingly crude.

So now I am to be a divorcée. I shall make it a fashionable status. In any event, I am well-established. I have had some faint thoughts of returning to the East, but always the fog blows them away. I am thinking that in a few years I will found my own company. I am doing some managing and plan to get quite rich. Doesn't that sound like a wonderful idea?

I can hardly believe you now have twins. I cannot imagine how you will manage and can only hope that your nanny is as competent as you believe her to be. I would love to see the little rascals. I'm sure they will be troupers like their parents.

I am off to Sacramento in a very few days for a brief run of one of the plays we will be taking on the road this summer. I've told you about my young friend Sylvia who lives there, well, she is newly engaged and has decided that she does not wish to attend college after all. I think this a great tragedy, that she has surrendered so wholly to her parents' designs for her life.

Freddy has worn me out and I am distressed for my young friend in Sacramento. With all this on my mind, I simply am not looking forward to traveling this year. I think what I would like to do is send my actor compatriots off to work and stay comfortably by the Bay myself, spending my time with the literati and with other actors too indolent to brave the rigors, and doing nothing but reading, planning, and preparing for the business of the autumn. Ah, well, if the mood of the moment is not happy, it will soon change. Pay no attention to my meanderings.

All my love to Arthur and to little Robert and Rosella.

Adela

Chapter Nine

Tina Freeman was first up on the blocks—that is, first up of anyone who might possibly win the role of Juliet. Elise sat way at the back of the theater, a few seats from Ralph Goldberg, so that they might whisper if need be but could mostly ignore each other's presence, wallowing, as Ralph put it, in the experience of the moment.

Tina moved onto the stage in her quasi-graceful manner: toes pointed, feet barely touching the ground. Elise found her intensely irritating, but tried to contain herself. She was supposed to be neutral, after all, if she would be any help to Ralph—as neutral as she could be when she too was angling for the part. Ralph leaned over a chair arm. "She looks like Juliet," he said.

Well, perhaps. She had long, dark hair, a decent build if too willowy, and she was fairly tall, which was all to the good, since the Romeo sent up by UC Berkeley was six-two. Ralph had needed someone younger looking than his stable of graduate students at Adela Honeycutt; none of the "house" men would do. The Romeo was an obnoxious sort, talented but stuck-up, rubbing his chin and making worried faces to call attention to his good looks and to his obliviousness to his good looks. Unfortunately, he really *was* handsome, and it didn't help that half the actresses were hanging on his every word or following him around like geese. (Some of the others, Elise had to admit, were following *her* around like geese.) At any rate, the two together—Romeo and Tina Freeman—were almost more than Elise could bear.

Tina gave a decent reading, all considered, which made Elise nervous. Would Ralph really choose Tina Freeman? There was the freshman angle—it wasn't fair to the sophomores and juniors. But also, Elise really felt that Tina would be unable to rise above her affectations, and Juliet was the opposite of affected. She was forthright and sensitive, and besides, someone capable of being stung so quickly by romance would not move as if she were waltzing through maple syrup.

Then Linda Martinez took the stage. Now here was someone who could be worked with; she could, in fact, be really good. If she could be coaxed to stand a bit differently, to thrust her shoulders back, if she modulated her words more fully to convey more than her usual ebullient self, if she were coerced to *be* Juliet…

"Elise Lemoine!"

"Elise! Your turn!"

"What?" she squawked. She hopped up from her seat, flustered, put down her clipboard, patted her hair. She'd been so involved with molding Linda Martinez into Juliet that she'd totally forgotten her own audition. She dashed up on the stage, got confused at her entrance, then waltzed out and flubbed her first line. "Can I start again?" she called into the darkness.

Ralph waved a weary hand; she could see his white fingers fluttering like doves above his head. This was stupid, she shouldn't even be wasting his time. He'd already decided not to use her. Distracted, she flubbed again, but drove on doggedly until the kiss, which Romeo delivered with great enthusiasm, lolling his tongue into her mouth as she tried discreetly to shove him away, finally emerging from his arms with a furious look that made Ralph call: "Come on, Elise, it can't be that bad! You look like you've bitten into a lemon!" and the whole theater rocked with laughter as Elise escaped back to her seat and her clipboard, her face burning.

"I'd say that was an unmitigated disaster," Elise muttered to Ralph when the last hopeful had her day behind the lights.

"Really? I thought there were several possibles."

"I meant me."

"Ah..." He couldn't restrain a grin. "I'd practice up on the kissing scene if I were you."

She tried to smash him with her clipboard but he hopped nimbly out of her way, his Puckish face alight with mischief.

Chapter Ten

Professor Rittola's office was cooler than it had been the last time Elise had come by. The tiny whirring noise in the corner explained it: a miniature fan. "I had to get one," Maiju apologized. "I had no idea it would be so hot out here."

"It isn't hot everywhere, not like this. It's probably about sixty-five in the City right now," Elise told her. "It'll cool down soon and start raining."

Maiju smiled, her midnight eyes alight. "Thank goodness. So—how is your project?"

"Fine. I'd like to thank you for helping me the other day with Dean Bankston."

Maiju nodded. She seemed curious but loath to ask. Finally she gave in to her impulse. "I wondered—she actually seemed not to like you."

"That's right," Elise said. She rocked her chair on its back legs and made a decision. Part of taking herself seriously meant presenting herself as she was. If Maiju didn't like it—well, at least Elise would know sooner than later, and drop what Frances kept calling nothing more than a fantasy. "She hates me because I'm gay. She hates all the lesbians."

Maiju said nothing for a moment. Then she nodded her head at Elise's chair. "Every time you do that I'm afraid you'll break your neck."

"You sound like my mother," Elise said, dropping forward and planting all six feet, including her own two, flat on the ground.

Maiju laughed. "Oh, I dearly hope not. I'm sure that's not welcome."

Elise was pleased. Maiju had not blanched; she'd even laughed. And there was no sign of the wariness or defensiveness which had marked their earlier meetings. Maiju actually seemed to be enjoying herself. Elise wondered if it would be pressing her luck to continue the conversation, but she quickly realized that once the subject was broached, she had an obligation to finish it; Maiju's career was more important than any pipe dream Elise might have of some-day getting her into bed. "In fact," Elise expanded, "the gay faculty members here have had to be more closeted than the students. They never give tenure to someone they discover is gay—even if she or he is very popular. It's all Bankston, too. She has blackball veto power or something."

"I see," Maiju said.

Elise could have dropped it there, but she went one step further. "Word to the wise, that's all."

Elise expected Maiju to retreat to questions about her project, but she didn't. "What makes you think I'm a lesbian, Elise?" she asked quietly.

Elise shrugged again. "I just know."

"I didn't think I was quite that obvious."

Elise smiled. At least they'd gotten that out of the way. "You're not obvious in the least."

"So am I to assume you're particularly perceptive and Dean Bankston will not be?"

Elise grinned. "I guess that's probably so."

"All right," Maiju said, "enough of this. Let's go back to your Adela paper. How are you doing with the letters?"

"Well, there's about two hundred of them. I'm wading through, trying to match up the dates with the diary entries so at least I'm reading in the same months. And I've begun a time line." She shook her head. "I've never done a project like this, so I'm not sure how to go about it. I'm making a checklist of subjects, kind of cataloging them so I could find specific topics? But I'm not sure I'm cataloging the right information."

"How can you be?" Maiju asked. "You're not certain what you're looking for. You're really working blind. Has a theme emerged?"

Elise gnawed on her lip, deep in thought. "Well, you know, I wanted to find out why she stopped acting. Or perhaps just why she founded the college. It's so odd how she stayed here like a recluse for twenty-two years until she died... It's especially unlikely after reading her early letters. She seems so vital, so full of life. I haven't a clue yet."

This time it was Maiju's turn to shrug. "Things change. Life changes us." She was growing remote again. Elise could almost measure the distance as she slipped away. She wanted to jump up and grab Maiju, shout at her to hold her in the present, in this office, but of course she could do nothing of the sort. "Would you like me to read more?" she asked, almost desperately. "I brought a couple with me."

Maiju showed a little spark. "Oh, yes, you could. That would be nice."

She listened as Elise read in a strong voice:

❦

20 April, 1859

Dearest Sylvie:

I am writing to thank you and your parents and your handsome fiance for your hospitality during my stay in Sacramento.

I was so glad you could all come to the opening night performance and delighted that you enjoyed your box seats. It was, after all, the least I could do. I wish only that you and I had had a moment alone together. Next time we meet I insist on it, and I know you wish it as much as I do.

Things are becoming extremely hectic here. I have taken on more management duties as well as a new role or two. And then of course there is the road tour this summer, but such is the life of a player. Dust and grime and arduous journeys —whereas your life will include none of that, lucky girl. Only an endless vista of propriety and cleanliness.

I am sure I will try my best to break away long enough to see you become Mrs. Walter Blake— what a solid, steady name he has—in June.

All my love,
Adela

"One more?" Elise asked.

Maiju nodded briefly, her short curls bouncing at her forehead. Then her face grew quiet and composed, her eyes abstracted as she prepared to listen.

❧

1 May, 1859

Sylvie, my dearest girl!

Please forgive me if I have hurt you! I did not mean for a moment that I would NOT be coming to your wedding. How could I possibly miss such an occasion? Of course I shall be there, and no, no, no! you have no reason to think I have grown cold to our friendship. Quite the contrary, only seeing you touch his hand brought tears to my eyes! I want to touch that soft and dimpled hand, to kiss you sweetly, and yet seeing you with your fiance, such a serious young man, made me afraid that you will have no time or heart or desire left for my presence in your life.

You say you fear that I will forget, have already forgotten you, but that will never happen. And I am heartened by your fears. You do love me, after all!

I was just today making arrangements for a replacement for the days I must be gone—we will be in Hangtown then, and it is not so very far away from Sacramento.

So I shall be there, because you are my sweet and adored Sylvie and I will not let you take such a step without my arm to lean upon.

Love,
Adela

Maiju made no comment on the letters, which Elise had chosen carefully, figuring a nudge in the right direction couldn't hurt.

"Perhaps you could copy all the letters for me, so I can keep up with you as you work on the project?"

"Of course," Elise said briskly, "though you do understand I'm using many more sources than just the letters."

"Oh, naturally. Sometime I'd like to see those playbills you were telling me about. You read so well, Elise. Have you always been so...sure of yourself?"

Elise almost exploded into laughter, but it would have been cruel, for Maiju was perfectly serious. "I don't really think of myself that way," she said. "I wish I *were* so sure."

"But you are," Maiju said. "Perhaps you just don't realize, or you can't see yourself objectively. Compared to most women your age, you have a great deal of poise."

"You should have seen me yesterday trying out for Juliet," Elise said with a smile. "I was anything but poised. I'm afraid I blew the part."

"Oh, I doubt that. But didn't you say you'd played Nora last year? Surely there are others who must star."

Elise nodded soberly. "You're right. But it's good practice to audition. I'll be doing enough of it in a few years." And secretly, of course, she had coveted the role. She felt a sharp stab of dismay at the thought that Ralph might actually give the part to Tina Freeman.

The discussion had drawn Maiju back in. Elise found her so wonderful when she was really there, when she wasn't slipping into the darkness that claimed her sometimes, that made her so sad... "Since you seem to know all, Elise," she said with her dark eyes twinkling, "where is an old hag like me to go to have a cocktail? Lulu's is clearly a student hangout. I know some of the faculty go to the pub, but I'd like to get off campus occasionally."

She lived at the Faculty House, Elise had discovered, which was unusual. Most of the faculty lived outside the Delta, driving the half-hour or forty-five minutes in to work. Perhaps she didn't drive. "Do you have a car?"

Maiju nodded. "I'm not entirely in the Stone Age. Yes, I have an old Volvo which managed to carry me out here from Connecticut. I'm sure it will go a few more miles. In fact, I intend to get an apartment in Crockett next semester, but I'd booked a room at the Faculty House when I was back East. I didn't come here to interview, so I wasn't sure of the situation. I thought the college was more remote than it actually is."

Elise's curiosity was rising by leaps and bounds. Why had Maiju not come out to interview for her job? Come to think of it, why had she come to Adela Honeycutt at all? The college was excellent, of course, as good as the women's colleges in the East—better, in fact, than some of the famous ones, which, having gone coed, were now admitting lesser qualified men in an attempt to equalize the sexes—but it still didn't have the almighty reputation of the Eastern schools.

No doubt Maiju had fallen prey to the tenure axe at Yale: hire new women faculty members every year, enough to keep up the ratio of female professors, but dismiss them before they qualified for tenure, replacing them with a new batch of women who were sure the same thing wouldn't happen to them. But why hadn't she simply gone elsewhere back East? Why pull up stakes and come out to California? There was always the lovelorn theory. Or perhaps Maiju simply thought her chance at a tenured position was best at Adela Honeycutt, in which case hearing that lesbians were Dean Bankston's *bête noire* must have been unpleasant news...

But Maiju was waiting patiently for the name of a decent bar. "The Sportsman's Club," Elise said. "It's not what it sounds. True, it's on the grounds of a duck hunting preserve, but it's really very nice. Good food, nice people. It's out on Highway 12 near Rio Vista. You can't miss it."

At Maiju's tentative smile, Elise thought perhaps she'd misunderstood. "I mean," she continued, "it's not gay or anything. Do you want names of bars in the City?"

"Oh, no," Maiju said, waving her off. "I have no interest in going to bars in San Francisco. No, this duck club seems right up my alley." She laughed. "A duck club. Imagine."

She was still chuckling as Elise left her office.

Chapter Eleven

10 October, 1859

Darling Sissy:

So happy to hear you and your little family are
doing well. I am well but worn to the bone from
the longest tour of all. Nevada City—does not
the romance of the Western names tempt you the
slightest little bit?—was wilder and woolier than
ever, there was a mix-up in the accommodations
and I nearly ended up sharing a room with a
commercial traveler from St. Louis. A very handsome one, I might add. But all went respectably,
at least in the case of the traveler! It is extremely
interesting, I must say, not having a husband
in tow. So many delightful companions can be
found on tour! And a woman must console herself
as best she can when husbands disappoint and
friends marry.

You asked about Sylvie's wedding. It was very
lavish. But the girl has married a stick of a man.
Handsome enough, with a lovely mustache, and
well-to-do, but I think he finds me somewhat
scandalous. Perhaps it is just because he is so
recently from the East, and not very sophisticated.

Possibly he is, like Sylvia's father, suspicious by nature. I kissed the bride, made her laugh with tales of San Francisco and sadly took my leave. I only hope he can make her happy, for she is the dearest child in the world. They went to England and France on their honeymoon. She found time to send me several notes along the way, and the notes sounded cheerful enough. They returned to Sacramento last month. I must answer her last letter. I want to, but I am saddened and find it hard to know what to say.

I think it is a great tragedy that all the world is not made up of players and plays. Other people, other lives, are so devastated by convention.

Yes, Freddy wrote to me that he has found work. I'm very glad for him, and I told him so by return mail. I suspect I shall not be hearing often from him in the future, and that divided by so many miles, our lives so separate, we will draw completely apart. But of course any news you have of him I would be eager to hear. I care about him, you see, it is only that I no longer care enough to make a great effort on his behalf. Am I hard? Cold? No, I don't think so. I have strong feelings. They have simply removed themselves from my husband.

Kiss the twins and Arthur for me.

Love,
Adela

"Elise, get out of those damned letters and talk to me!"

Elise sighed. "Do you know how much I have to do, Frances?"

Frances had swept into Elise's room wearing a long silk dress of the palest gray-rose, which set off her hair and eyes perfectly. Elise sat up with a start. Frances looked incredible. "What's going on?" Elise asked, knowing that her question had just axed a half-hour from her tight study schedule. Still, Frances was her friend.

"Do you think this looks nice?"

"It's unbelievable. You look yummy enough to eat."

"Down, girl." But then Frances's smile faded. "I was wearing this yesterday." She dug her toes into the shag remnant that Elise had bought to put on the linoleum floor next to her bed. Then Frances heaved a big sigh. Elise waited. "I went out with Don," she expanded.

"Yesterday," Elise coaxed, reminding herself that she had a quiz in Italian the next morning. "Don is the married man."

"To the Perpetual Headache."

Silence. Elise stared out her window. It was finally cooling down. Frances grasped the neckline of her dress and tugged hard. Nothing happened. "It's hard to rend clothing," she noted.

"Don left you," Elise concluded, if only to take Frances's mind off the gorgeous but defenseless dress.

Frances nodded miserably. "I hate him."

"That seems sensible."

"But I also love him."

"That doesn't."

Frances glared at her and Elise shrugged. "Well, it's true. The jerk left you, and how lovable is that? But—" Elise decided she should just plunge in. "Part of it is you, Frances. Don is married. M-A-R—"

"I know how to spell."

"You don't, though. It spells 'off-limits.' It spells 'heart-break.' "

Frances said nothing. She glared at the rug, which, with its various-length tufts of red and orange, clashed horribly with her dress.

"Let's get out of here," Elise urged, oppressed at even the thought of her Italian quiz. "Come on. Let's go to Lulu's."

"Lulu's is such a scum-dive."

"That's why it's perfect. Come on, Frances."

Frances grudgingly dragged herself along after Elise. She climbed into the Mustang and stared out the window as Elise circled Honeycutt Island to get to the car bridge and then drove back to Lulu's on the mainland. She sat in the car disconsolately until Elise pried her out. The odd couple, Elise thought as they walked across the parking lot: Elise in her faded jeans and jungle-print blouse, Frances in her gown. They had gotten their beers and sat down before Elise noted the other two early denizens of Lulu's: Jamie and Tina Freeman.

"Charming," Frances remarked, nodding at the two lovebirds huddled together in the farthest booth.

Elise felt her stomach hollow out, as if a small-scale grenade had just exploded inside. She was immediately enraged at herself. Why did Jamie still affect her like this? It was asinine.

"A big person would walk over there and say hi," Frances said.

"I'm not that big a person."

They gulped at their beers nervously and had to go back for more. Elise avoided looking at Jamie and Tina, who were now practically making out in the booth, for her benefit, she was certain. Tina didn't know her function was to make Elise jealous. Well, maybe she was jealous, but she didn't wish herself in Tina's shoes. "I'm more envious that Jamie has someone," she admitted to Frances.

"That's funny," Frances said, "because I don't think Jamie believes she does have someone. You're a challenge to her. Tina isn't."

Elise stared at her. "If you understand that, how could you possibly push Jamie at me?"

Frances shrugged. "Relationships aren't all apple pie and cherry sodas. Oh, but I forgot. You're the Big Book in the Sky person. Ms. Romantic."

"Just because you've been disappointed doesn't mean you have to attack me."

"No, you're right. You're focused on a wonderful dream—you and Maiju Rittola walking down the aisle hand in hand."

"So what's so impossible about that?" Elise asked, even as she wondered if that really were her dream. It was hard to maintain a fantasy about someone who was back-pedaling away as fast as she could.

Frances began ticking off items on her fingers. "One, she isn't interested. Two, she's old. Three, she's about as accessible as the inside of a beehive. Four, she isn't interested."

Elise stared into her beer. "Gee, Frances," she said weakly, "you really know how to show a girl a good time."

Frances shook her head. "Sorry, kid. Come on, let's blow this scene, take a drive. Besides, I want you to pay attention to me. I'm the one who got left this week."

So they left Lulu's, and it wasn't too strange that on their meandering path the Mustang strayed several times in the direction of the Sportsman's Club—but Maiju's old Volvo was not in evidence.

Chapter Twelve

Elise decided it was absolutely time to buckle down. It was, in fact, almost too late to buckle down. She had to stop driving past the Sportsman's Club. She had to stop consoling Frances, who seemed more broken up about this Don guy than she'd ever been about anybody in the past. Since Elise had never even met him, it all sounded like a strange dream, but it was clearly no dream to Frances. Elise could hear her crying at night through the paper-thin walls.

Start working, she told herself. She had already done four hours of Italian homework this morning, which was supposed to make up for days of inattention and her lousy grades on the two quizzes she hadn't studied for. Yesterday she'd completed her Pirandello paper, though now that she thought about it, she could make some changes. Forget it, her inner voice commanded harshly. You have too many things to do! And anyway, it was getting pretty interesting between Adela and Sylvie:

❦

12 May, 1860

Dear Sylvie:

Please accept my apologies for not answering your letters sooner—I promise to do better. Sylvie, sweet, I am your friend forever, and you must believe that. I know you will forgive me, although I have no excuse except a difficulty with your new life—I wonder, always, how it will change you.

So, you are expecting a child. How wonderful for you and Walter. You must take very good care of yourself. I will be in Sacramento for three weeks in June and cannot wait to see you and talk to you. I want to be sure that you are doing well and are happy and healthy!

I have decided that, despite the hardships, there is much to love about the summer's tour of the mines. I have invested in one or two of the touring companies myself, so I expect to do quite well. Also, the miners are really our best audiences, not spoiled like our cosmopolitan San Franciscans. They adore us! How can one fault them for that? (And you, my love? Do you adore us?)

We'll be doing several melodramas and comedies on our tour, too, everyone loves those. I mean melodramas and comedies written by more contemporary playwrights. Although I must say, I don't think very many of those will have Mr. Shakespeare's longevity.

So, prepare for me in June, sweet friend. We will talk for hours and I will hold the hand on which you wear a ring.

Your loving
Adela

.

❦

7 September, 1860:

Dear Sissy,

This was a summer of artistic and financial success and of great sadness as well.

74

My sweet young friend, Sylvia—it was dreadful. When I arrived at her home in June I was told she was too ill to see me. She had miscarried just the week before. But I sent flowers and a pleading note to her sickroom and a day later, she sent for me.

She was very pale and very sad. I had brought a ring for her little finger, a lovely topaz the color of her hair. She wept when she saw me and she wept even harder when she saw the ring. I held her in my arms for a very long time. Until her husband, Walter, arrived and asked me to leave her to rest for a while. She did not want me to go, but she was very tired, so I complied.

I visited her every day and every day I held her, stroked her poor pale hand, listened to her sadness for her child, her regret that she had not given a much-desired son to her husband.

I told her she would have other children and that some of them might, with luck, be daughters as beautiful and intelligent as she and as talented as I! It was good to make her laugh. But she does not believe she will ever have a child.

When I left Sacramento she was much improved, and is quite well now. But there was still a sadness in her last letter I would give a great deal to be able to cure, and she says she wishes she could see me more often. Perhaps I will try to trek to Sacramento more, just to visit. Although I no longer have to meet her father each time I go, I care as little for Walter. Oh, I suppose he's not as bad as all that. She says he is a gentle and generous husband. I must learn to appreciate that in him. But the man has no sense of humor, and my darling Sylvie needs laughter in her precious life!

I am sorry that you are seeing less of Freddy these days, but he sounded very full of himself when I last heard and I expect he will do perfectly well.

Love,
Adela

2 March, 1861

Darling Sylvie:

How interesting—no, I have not read Mrs. Stowe's newest work. *The Minister's Wooing*— what a clever title. I did of course read *Uncle Tom's Cabin* several years ago but I am obviously not nearly so *au courant* in literary matters as you. I promise I will read it and thank you for sending it.

I'm glad you enjoyed the set of Shakespeare's Comedies I sent to you, and of course it was not too expensive. If one is going to buy books, I believe, one ought to have gold leaf on the covers.

You asked whether I knew of Susan B. Anthony? Yes, I've heard of her. One of our music hall comedians took a turn at her, prancing about in bloomers, looking harsh, and demanding certain body parts for her own. But I have heard she is really very intelligent. Women's rights—my dear Sylvia, one takes what one can! But you're quite right, I would like, I think, to vote. Men don't seem to do it very well.

I miss you so desperately. I'm glad you are feeling happier now. Do you and Walter never plan to come to San Francisco? I will, I promise, visit you next month. If you only lived here, we could see each other every day. Vain hope, I know, but a dream perhaps the kinder gods will hear.

Love always,
Adela

Could Adela be in love with Sylvie? It certainly seemed possible. Something was tapping Elise's memory, trying to gain entrance. What? she asked irritably. Something to do with Sylvie's name? Blake. Was that it? No, that was her married name. Muttering to herself, Elise rifled through the stacks of letters that were sitting in piles all over her room.

Maiden name...Woodruff! Elise sat back on her heels. Why hadn't she noticed that before? Woodruff Hall was the name of the original campus house, the first administration building, which had been redone in the '60s as a series of offices and classrooms. Was Adela a lesbian? Was that why she'd left San Francisco and retreated to the Delta? Had her affair with Sylvie been discovered?

But hang on, Elise cautioned herself. Adela had been married to Freddy, although he was long gone by this time. Sylvie was not only married but she also seemed devoted to her husband, or at least to the idea of giving him children. Adela and Sylvie barely found time to see each other, and there was really nothing to indicate they were having an affair, though Elise doubted they'd put that in the letters. But the husband was around, after all, throwing Adela out of Sylvie's room! On the other hand, why would Adela leave San Francisco if she were a lesbian? Surely the City would offer an easier life for a sexual outlaw?

Still, how amazing—and distressing—it would be if she had inadvertently discovered that Adela was a lesbian. The college would not be pleased. Dean Bankston would blow a gasket. The discovery might even reflect badly on Maiju, since she'd been the faculty advisor on the project. Elise frowned, but then reminded herself that these Victorian ladies were always rambling on about how "fond" they were of one another. It probably meant nothing, she thought. She stared off into the middle distance beyond her window, where tall sycamores sliced into the sky. Planted by Adela?

Elise thought she would have liked to meet Adela Honeycutt. Whether Adela was gay or straight, living as a single woman in those times took a lot of courage.

Chapter Thirteen

"Elise?" She sat back on her heels when Ralph Goldberg called her name. She'd been crawling around in the basement of the theater, making notes on a now-filthy pad of paper, inventorying the boxes and closets of costumes which had been moldering down there for ages. When she stood up and fought her way through debris to reach the bottom of the stairs, he burst into laughter: "Jesus, look at you!"

"I can't," she said drily. "But I gather the sight is amusing."

He came clattering down the metal staircase. "You don't look like my star performer at the moment, let's put it that way. Now I wanted to tell you this personally, that's why I'm down here."

"Tell me what?" Elise asked, but she already knew. He had chosen someone else to play Juliet.

"I picked Linda Martinez," he said. "Partially because of your ingenue remark. You were right."

He was just trying to butter her up with these compliments. "Was it the kiss?"

"Hell, no, I was just teasing you. You were fine."

"Then—"

"Elise, you don't look like Juliet. You're too old."

"Too old! I'm twenty! Linda Martinez is nineteen!"

"I know that, but Linda Martinez maybe doesn't have as much to think about as you do, know what I mean?"

"No, I don't know, so you'd better explain."

Ralph sighed. "Oh, Jesus… I can't really put my finger on it—"

"Try."

"You're too mature. It's a wonderful way to be—the only way, as far as I'm concerned—but it just doesn't work for Juliet. She's supposed to be an innocent."

"This is a nice way of saying I look ravaged," Elise concluded. "Jaded. Spent. Tawdry." She threw a handful of metal hangers against a nearby concrete wall.

Ralph winced at the noise. "Elise, Elise, come on, now…"

"Is this because I'm gay, Ralph? All lesbians are sophisticates? I've heard that line before, you know, from Dean Bankston. She's always saying she doesn't mind the dykes as long as their presence doesn't offend the poor naive farm girls. What about the poor naive dykes? Does every lesbian spring full-blown from San Francisco and New York?"

They had never said the words, always skirting the issue, but Ralph was perfectly willing to dive right in. "Your not playing Juliet has nothing to do with your sexual orientation, Elise. My other top pick was Tina Freeman, who I've noticed hangs around with the gay crowd."

"Tina Freeman is an idiot."

"Agreed, which is why she didn't get the part. But that should allay your suspicions about my straight bias, okay?"

"Okay," Elise said. She had suddenly run out of steam. She sat down on the bottom step, laid the palms of her hands against her eyes and pressed gently, then realized she had just deposited about a half-century's worth of dust all over her face. "I'm filthy," she said. She couldn't remember ever feeling so miserable.

"Elise, would you like to go out to dinner?"

"I tell you I'm filthy and you want me to go out to dinner?"

"I thought we could discuss the coming schedule."

"Maybe later, Ralph. Besides, you don't need to placate me. I'll be all right."

He nodded, his face solemn. "You must realize that you're my most important actor. Juliets are a dime a dozen. Elises don't come along very often." He patted her shoulder awkwardly and clomped up the metal stairs. She heard the fire door slam shut at the top.

"Damn!" she screamed. Then she shouted again because it made a very satisfying echo in the big basement.

Too young for Maiju, too old for Juliet. Too naive for Maiju, too jaded for Juliet. Maybe she could write a country-western song. "Too Young To Be So Old"? Sounded good. She tried it out for a few moments, crooning the words, then suddenly heard herself. What the hell's wrong with you, Elise, she asked. Get out of this dung heap and go do something, anything!

Chapter Fourteen

Elise escaped to her room and to Adela's letters. She had two copies of them now, the set she was working from and another—the thick envelope was still in her car, where she tossed it on the way to a class—that she'd made to give Maiju.

She hoped that Maiju wouldn't compare her, the aspiring actor, to the amazingly strong and competent Adela. Elise was painfully aware that Adela, in spite of to the severe restraints put on women during that tiresome age, had managed to accomplish a great deal more than Elise. Of course, Adela was older…but still. Ever since she'd decided to stop sleeping around and make her life more meaningful, Elise thought with annoyance, the tenor of her days had gone from shallow to stultifying, sordid to stagnant. It was hard to paint this as an improvement, even to the part of her that wanted desperately to believe that she was moving forward spiritually. It didn't help that her early teen years had been so active, between modeling and prancing about from community stage shows to school productions. Now she felt like a washout, her life finished at twenty!

Frances's only advice had been that Jamie was always a nice pick-me-up for a girl wanting her ego massaged. (This was said with a revolting leer. Elise had slammed the bathroom door so hard that she was afraid for a moment that she'd cracked the wood.)

But to take her mind off her troubles, she would turn to Adela, who had problems of her own:

❦

9 May, 1862

Dear Sissy:

I was much grieved to receive your news of Freddy. His death is a great shock to me, I discover, although I have hardly thought of him lately except to be glad that he was happy and doing well. I found myself weeping copious and bitter tears for the young sweet man I married.

And to die in such a way...to end one's life beneath the wheels of a carriage must have been painful. Still, I console myself by assuming he fell beneath those wheels because he was drunk—although you were too kind to say so—in which case the pain would have been ameliorated. A sad loss to all of us.

At least he did not die on some filthy battlefield, we can be grateful for that. We hear so much about the war here, although we are so far away. How much more immediate and frightening it must be for you. Abolition is the best of causes, but I don't really believe any man has ever gone to war to free another man. I think there must be business reasons here—everything is business—and that the men who go do so because they are seeking glory or spoils. The most naive and the most cynical. Like the gunfighters we see so often here in the West.

I can only wish for the slaves to be truly freed and the battles to end soon.

So, Arthur is a theater owner! I am managing the Lumiere, a new theater in Portsmouth Square, and what fun I'm having—taking all the best roles for myself! Of course I am only joking. I am trying to kidnap the child star, Lotta Crabtree, from her music hall and not having a great deal of success. She is thirteen now and I think could create a sensation on the legitimate stage with her enormous singing and dancing and acting talents.

Are Robert and Rosella to be child stars? They are three now, isn't that so? Do they know many songs? What a charming act they could make, he in blue and she in pink.

Write soon with happier news. I cannot help but think—and this is very painful—that if Freddy had stayed here with me he would be alive. Could I have done more to make him happy? Sadly, I do not think so.

Love,
Adela

ॐ

Virginia City
3 August, 1862

Darling Sylvie:

Yes, I, too, wish you were here with me—although I am not sure how you would take to Virginia City!

There is the most wonderful journalist here recently come out from the East—I think you would enjoy him. He is learned and very amusing. His name is Samuel Clemens but he calls himself Mark Twain—something to do with his life on the Mississippi River. He writes about everything—including us players. He gave us a lovely notice on our Macbeth and has written a special little piece on me, as well. I have enclosed both for your amusement—and of course to impress you with my importance, and make you jealous of those who are here to share these little triumphs with me.

How I loved our walk along the river together, just the two of us, hand in hand. How sweet to be close to you, to talk of love and trees and poetry and paintings. To kiss your plump but too-pale cheek. If you would only come to San Francisco! I long to show you how it has grown and changed since you last were there.

But I suppose I must be content with our brief and infrequent visits. Must I? I am not!

It seems we have known each other a long time now, yet our friendship, unlike so many others, is always new.

I have been thinking lately about how you wanted to go to college—and how there were so few schools where you could go. I remember you telling me you had no desire to go to a normal school and learn to be a poor teacher, and how your father guided you through the classics when you clamored for an education beyond music and sewing and the writing of pretty verses.

I wonder how your life would have been different if you'd had the educational opportunities the slowest boys are privy to. I wonder, too, how my life would have been different if my choices had been wider. I think I would have been a player in any case—but perhaps a better-educated one.

Perhaps we could have gone to college and been scholars together. Except that I am older than you by some eight years, so I suppose that would not have happened in any case.

Well, my beloved Sylvie, excuse my might-have-beens. I had a snifter of very fine brandy this evening and it has quite gone to my head. I hope I will dream of you tonight, and dream that you have come to me and lie sweetly sleeping in my bed.

> All my love,
> Adela

❧

2 January, 1863

Dearest Sissy:

Forgive me for being such a poor correspondent. I think of you always but summer was a whirlwind and I am feeling wearied by a rainy and chill winter. Writing is not enough. I wish you and Arthur would come and sweep me away to a Pacific Island. But you will not. Nor will my dear young friend Sylvia, who languishes in Sacramento with her great provider. I wish she were bolder and more daring, but then she would not be my Sylvie… If I were a man I would save her from a life of boredom. But no man or creature of any sex comes to save me, even though there are many who favor me with their attentions for either my power or my beauty.

Are you scandalized by my thoughts? I hope not. I am, just a little.

I am happy here. I have so many clever friends, and, I admit, some who have been more. But Love, Love is missing. Or something that must be love. I do not miss Freddy, I am ashamed to say, and never really did. Perhaps you should not show this letter to Arthur; he will be incensed for the sake of his old, dead friend.

I have lost Lotta Crabtree to Maguire! He snatched her up and into the Eureka Minstrel Hall while my Lumiere was being repaired after a fire. Did I write you about the fire? Good heavens, I think I did, but in a letter I somehow never mailed that was left in some dreadful hotel in the Gold Country! Well, no one was hurt and my darling theater is whole again, but at the time it was terrifying. We barely saved the place! Sometimes I think every theater in this city is destined to burn, but it never matters because a new Phoenix always rises from the ashes. Except that Maguire is the one who is making a profit on the Crabtree's popularity, which I worked so hard to foster. Wretched man. My only consolation is that I think she will not stay with him long. I think she will soon go East and then perhaps on to Europe. She is growing up.

I admit that while I admired and enjoyed her talents I never was particularly fond of her; some of the child actors are sweet enough, but they are never quite children, either. But the profits! Oh, well. I have now taken over management of a new theater called the Bijou. I have a financial stake in several others and I am building a lovely

new house on the hill, and from my parlor window
I will be able to see the ships arrive in the Bay
with their travelers from the East.

My love to Arthur and the children,

Your friend
Adela

Elise turned back to the letter to Sylvie and reread the
final paragraph. "Sweetly sleeping in my bed" indeed. That
seemed far beyond the fulsomeness of Victorian ladies. If
she were right and Adela was a lesbian, there'd be hell to
pay with Dean Bankston.

Frances pounded on the door. Sick of Frances constantly
bursting in when she was studying, Elise had taken the
precaution of locking it from her side. "What's with you,
Lemoine?" Frances blustered the moment Elise pried herself
from the bed and opened the door. She peered around
suspiciously. "Well, this is a big disappointment. I thought
you had an entire chorus line in here at least."

"Give it a rest," Elise suggested.

"You've got to give *it* some fun, honey, or it might
forget why it's there, get what I mean?"

"Why does everyone ask if I 'get what they mean'
when they've just insulted me?"

Frances patted her shoulder. "Poor Elise. Things aren't
going well, are they? Oh, I forgot, Ralph is on the phone."

"What?"

"Yeah, on the hall phone. Guess he doesn't have your
private number." She giggled. Elise didn't have a phone.
Elise shot her a look and dashed out into the hall where the
receiver hung halfway down the wall, dangling forlornly
at the end of its cord.

"Hi, Ralph. Sorry, my roommate's kind of a flake."

"Uh-huh. Listen, Elise, ya know why I wanted you
to come out to dinner with me?" He didn't give her time
to answer. "I really wanted to talk to you about more
than the schedule. What I wanted—see, you've been my
ad hoc production assistant for the past year with no title
and no recognition."

Great, she thought. She would appear in the program in tiny letters underneath the costume designer and makeup artist. Elise Lemoine, Girl Gofer.

"So what I wanted to do," he was continuing, "is to give you what you deserve, which is to be my assistant director for the three productions this year. I know you'll be starring in one, and we'll reduce your work load then. But on the other two, we'll work together on pretty much everything—casting, directing, interpretation... And part of it will be pulling together the workshop people too. It's a big job." He sounded uncertain. "I don't know how much time you'll have. This can't interfere with your class work or the dean will have my head."

Elise had nearly stopped breathing. She hadn't known how much she wanted this until she'd heard him say the words. Her disappointment over Juliet had been reduced to less than nothing. But was that why...

"Ralph, you don't feel you have to do this—"

"Do you really *want* to do it?" he interrupted. "I was afraid to ask. I think it'd be fantastic for your career. You're a magnificent actor. But versatility is the key in today's theater. If you can handle whatever job comes along, you're going to stay in theater. You'll be able to earn your keep. And you'll understand what it takes to make a show work so that other people can earn a living too. You're going to make a real contribution."

She was dizzy. She slid down the wall and rested on her heels. Frances poked her head out the door and raised her eyebrows inquisitively. Elise waved her away. "Elise?"

"Yes, Ralph."

"What do you think?" His voice was anxious.

"I think I'm walking on a cloud."

"Oh!" he laughed. "I'm so glad. Look, I'll see you tomorrow, all right? We can talk more then."

Frances grinned at her. "Well, I don't know what's happened, but at least you look more like the old Elise! Celebration in order? Oysters on the half-shell? C'mon, kid, let's rock!"

Chapter Fifteen

The oysters on the half-shell turned into giant hamburgers and fries at Lulu's and the celebration degenerated into lamentations about Don and his cursed infidelity (not to his wife, of course, to Frances), but Elise couldn't have cared less. Finally something was going right! And she had always believed that once begun, good things tended to come in a flood...

"I cannot believe we are doing this once again," Frances said. She had been almost silent during their apparently nonsensical route after they'd left the bar, though she noted acidly that if they hoped to get back to school before Christmas, it might be best to head straight for the Sportsman's Club rather than wandering about for hours in its vicinity.

Released from any further need for pretense, Elise spun the Mustang into a screeching U-turn on the levee, nearly spilling them into the water. "I just have a feeling," she said.

"You've had a feeling for days. Maybe it's premenstrual."

"You're such a grouch, Frances."

"It's Don that's upset me. Why did he leave me?"

"For the eternal headache he's married to," Elise answered.

"Have you ever noticed you think your love life is serious while mine is hilarious?" A sharp anger was building underneath Frances's bantering tone. "Shall we have a little discussion about that indisputable fact?"

But Elise was saved from an argument by the sight of the old Volvo parked in the shadow of a tree. "She's here!" she cried.

"Oh, so what? Besides, how many old Volvos are there in Northern California? Only about twenty-five or thirty thousand."

"No, it's hers, I'm almost sure."

Elise cruised by to make certain, her tires crunching across the gravel. Frances peered into the gloom.

"Well, there's someone in that car, girl, so if it's hers, it's her, if you get my meaning."

"What's she doing in there?"

"How the hell should I know? Go ask her."

"Frances!"

"Elise, you have been circling this place like a goddamn vulture for days. Now you've finally got some meat. Go find out why she's sitting in a dark car in a dark parking lot underneath a willow tree at midnight."

"All right, I will," Elise said, her voice determined. She jammed the slowly rolling Mustang to a stop, pulled on the parking brake, and hopped out of the car. "Wish me luck."

"Luck," Frances said, rolling her eyes.

Elise approached Maiju's car cautiously, afraid that the professor might not be alone. But no, it was just Maiju, and she appeared to be...sleeping? Slowly Maiju raised her head, as though she'd heard Elise's footsteps. It was time to say something so she wouldn't be frightened—"Hi, Professor Rittola. I was driving by and noticed you sitting in the car." Not that it would be possible to see her from the highway, but maybe Maiju wouldn't know that. "Are you okay?" Elise leaned close to the half-open window.

Maiju shook her head ruefully. "Oh, Elise." She smiled crookedly. "I'm afraid I drank a bit too much. I thought I'd just sit here for a bit and wait 'til it wears off. It scares me how fast people drive on these two-lane roads."

Since Elise had just been doing seventy in a forty-five-mile zone, she understood. "Well, listen, I'm here with my roommate. Why don't I drive your car back to the college, and she can drive mine?"

"Oh, I can't ask you to do that! Your roommate might be angry—"

"No, honestly, she won't be. We were just driving around, and we were on our way back anyhow. It's no trouble."

"Well...all right. If it won't bother you. I'm terribly sorry."

"Oh, don't apologize," Elise said. She took off running to her Mustang, hoping Maiju wouldn't change her mind in the interim. She skidded to a stop and poked her head in Frances's window. "She's uh—kind of under the weather."

"Is that a nice way of saying she's loaded?" Frances swiveled around in her seat to peer at Maiju. "Well, vulture, here's your big chance. The lady's vulnerable. Turn on the charm, sweep her off her feet—"

"No."

"Why not?"

"Because if we go to bed together I don't want her to be able to put it off to booze."

Frances regarded her quizzically. "You really are in love with her, aren't you?"

But Elise was getting impatient. "Listen, hand me that envelope from the back seat—it's for her. And I told her I'd drive her back and you would take the Mustang."

"Oh, you did, did you? What if I don't want to take the Mustang?"

Elise was hopping from foot to foot anxiously, thinking that as each second passed, Maiju would become more certain that she was causing trouble and that she would call out to Elise to forget it, to go on home, she'd be fine...

Frances reached back for the envelope—Maiju's copies of Adela's letters—and handed it to Elise. "For god's sake, here, take it. And stop dancing around and get over there!

But if you're not back in our room in thirty minutes, I'll be tossing rocks at the faculty house windows." At Elise's panicked look, she said, "Just kidding, dopey. Go!"

Chapter Sixteen

By the time Elise returned, Maiju had clambered over to the passenger side of her Volvo and inserted the key in the ignition. Not so drunk after all, Elise thought. She had to rap on the glass to gain entry to the car, however; Maiju had cautiously locked herself in when she'd decided to nap under the willow tree.

"All set?" Elise inquired brightly as she sank into the bucket seat of the Volvo. Christ, I sound like a stewardess! Cool it, Lemoine. She was nervous, her scalp tingling, hands sweating, like a preadolescent on her first date. She couldn't remember being so nervous since...maybe the beginning of Jamie, when she'd thought such an accomplished dyke would find her hopelessly naive, no matter what her other attractions. She'd practically hero-worshipped Jamie at first. No wonder, after that torturous relationship with guilt-ridden Ruth. Why am I thinking of Jamie and Ruth? she snapped at herself. Pay attention!

Meanwhile, she'd managed to pull out of the parking lot onto the main highway. In her rearview mirror, she saw the Mustang's headlights flash on, and then pull behind her. Damn that Frances. I'll get rid of her... Elise slowed down to a decorous twenty-five miles per hour, which

Frances could only bear for thirty seconds. She powered by like a wild animal glimpsed in the shadows.

"I'm not this timorous," Maiju said, sitting up. "You can drive a little faster."

"Okay," Elise said agreeably. She stole a glance to her right. Maiju was smiling enigmatically—or at least it looked enigmatic to Elise, who didn't trust her own judgment when it came to Maiju Rittola. There did seem to be amusement playing around her lips, crinkling the corners of her eyes. Finns often looked like that, Elise remembered from her family's trip to Scandinavia. The Norwegians were gloomy, as if life had played them a dirty trick and they were adding up the injustices; the Swedes were open and expansive; the Finns knew life's joke but forged ahead anyway with great relish, winking at each other occasionally—any other response was taking oneself too seriously, which anyone who knew the joke would never do. At first, this gallows humor seemed at odds with the tremendous natural beauty of the country, but after awhile it fit right in. Since her trip, Elise had noticed that the transplants, like Maiju, had not lost their razor edge.

Maiju was now gazing at her frankly. "You're awfully deep in thought."

"Yes. I was thinking about Finland. I went there with my family when I was sixteen."

Maiju stretched in her seat, her arm coming close to almost graze Elise's breast. Had she done that on purpose?

"I've never been," Maiju said. "Isn't it odd how the ones who came here never went back to visit? None of them. They left when they were so young." She pondered as the car cruised along the river road towards Honeycutt Island. "At first I thought they couldn't afford to go. But they could. In dollars and cents they could. But they were not frivolous people. They knew they couldn't visit a dream, so they believed it was too costly to go back. But by not going, they paid in a different manner..." Her voice changed, became harder. "After awhile, you see that everything costs." She stared straight ahead at the dark road. "Everything."

A shiver passed across Elise's shoulders. She fumbled for the blinker, signaling a left turn for the bridge to Honeycutt Island. What happened to you, Maiju Rittola? You are not much older than I am but something terrible—

The crinkles were back at the corners of Maiju's eyes, and her voice held a hint of apology, as if she'd been embarrassingly self-indulgent. "So tell me, Elise, anything earthshaking in your life lately?"

Sure, Elise thought. I'm sitting in your car, driving you to the Faculty House. That's pretty damn incredible. If someone had told me at dinner that at 12:30 a.m., I'd be driving you home, I—"Not really," Elise said. "I didn't get Juliet. Linda Martinez was chosen."

"Oh! Are you terribly disappointed?"

Elise avoided that question. "Ralph made me his assistant director. He's never had one before."

"Well, that's wonderful!" Maiju said with more enthusiasm than Elise could quite encompass. "I think that's so much better than playing Juliet, which is an insipid role at best. Besides, you're much too mature to play Juliet."

Elise's heart surged. I am? You don't think I'm a little kid? Then she was amused. When Ralph said she was too mature, she was plunged into the deepest depression; when Maiju said it, she was practically out of the car and dancing across the bridge.

"You'll learn much more directing," Maiju continued. "I can't emphasize enough that you should do as many different things in college as you can. It's when you should experiment, find what you like. There's plenty of time later to rope yourself down to one discipline." She glanced at Elise. "Uh-oh, now I've gotten on my professorial horse, haven't I? I'm terribly sorry."

By this time, Elise was pulling up in front of the Faculty House. She was not offended in the least. In fact, she was fairly certain that Maiju would invite her in to discuss all these marvelous ventures she should be trying. "Park it right in front," Maiju said. "Everybody's gone for the weekend. No one will care."

Elise pulled the car in front of the big brown-shingled house with its wide front porch. Maiju turned to her, her hand outstretched. Elise shook it awkwardly, feeling dazed. "Thank you so much for saving me from an uncomfortable few hours."

Elise's heart sank, and she knew her eyes, never very guarded, had telegraphed her disappointment. Maiju caught it and faced it head-on. "Oh, it's so late, Elise. Both of us are tired." She thought for a moment. "I'll tell you what. Why don't we have dinner together tomorrow? We could go into town. Or—we could return to the Sportsman's Club and have one of those steaks you mentioned. How about it?" Her bright eyes were glistening with excitement.

"Of course," Elise said. "Yes, that would be wonderful." She handed the keys to Maiju and smiled at her. She felt brave, hopeful. She couldn't imagine waiting until tomorrow. Their eyes had locked. How long could they sit here gazing at each other before something happened? Elise felt—or was it only imagination?—that Maiju was leaning closer and closer. She could almost feel Maiju's breath on her cheeks. She sensed Maiju's hand beginning to rise, as if to touch Elise's breasts, or her lips...surely she wasn't imagining that, was she? But then Maiju twisted away abruptly and opened her car door. Elise confusedly followed suit. This could be the end, Lemoine, her pessimistic side warned. Maiju might decide it's too dangerous and call off the dinner. Death in the family. Or simply tell the truth. No personal involvements with students. Do something now, Lemoine, or she walks out of your life. But Elise couldn't. She stood at the bottom of the steps and watched Maiju ascend the broad stairs, unlock the heavy walnut door, and disappear inside the Faculty House. She had not looked back.

Chapter Seventeen

While she waited for Maiju's phone call, Elise spent the day working on her paper on Jean Genet's *The Balcony*. She'd also had time for a few missives from Adela, and things were getting interesting indeed:

2 September, 1863

Dearest Sissy:

The famous and notorious Ada Isaacs Menken has come to San Francisco and has captivated us all! The Jewess is lovely, intelligent, and a dreadful rascal—my friend Mark Twain calls her "a manly young female," and of course she has had several husbands—do you know how many? She will not tell me!

She performed her Mazeppa—have you ever seen her in it?—from the poem by Byron. She was incomparable as the Tartar prince, astride her horse up there on the stage—unfortunately, Maguire's stage, at his Opera House. But she has promised to appear in my theater some day when she returns. So magnificent on that horse, and she writes such lovely verses. She likes to spend her time with Bret Harte and his crew—smoking cigars, dressing as a man, and visiting brothels! She invited me to join them and I have once or twice. I played cards with the madame. I have no idea what Ada did.

What fun she is! But now, alas, she is off to the Comstock and I feel that a light has gone out from our city.

Tell me more about the twins! They sound brilliant, and of course I didn't mean what I said about child actors.

Love and kisses,
Adela

❦

12 September, 1863

Darling Sylvie:

My dearest beloved! How could you believe it of me for even a moment? I adore Ada, but she is a scoundrel, an imp from Hell, and besides that she has gone away. I could never love her more than you, my friendship with her could never replace ours. My silly muffin of a Sylvie.

I told you of her escapades to amuse you—as she amused me. Am I to languish here unamused? While you lead your quiet life in Sacramento... If I do not have you here by my side, if I cannot stroke your hand, your cheek, if I cannot walk with you and know you are my very own sweet Sylvie, would you have me languishing alone, without friends? I do not think so.

Have you read Mrs. Howe's divine poem, Battle Hymn of the Republic? I hear it is becoming very popular in the East as the Union's own anthem. I know she has written some plays and other things, but I am not familiar with them, nor is anyone else I know. The poem was published last year in the Atlantic Monthly, and I've enclosed that magazine page for you. Very stirring.

I hope this letter soothes your perturbation with me. Sometimes I think you will drive me mad with tenderness from afar.

For God's sake, come to San Francisco and visit me!

Love always,
Adela

❦

15 June, 1864

Dear Sissy:

So, you have seen our Lotta Crabtree perform at last. In a variety program, you say, at Niblo's Saloon? She had, as I wrote you, been dipping her dainty toes in the legitimate stage here at Maguire's, and doing a good job of it, too. But the magic of the East calls to so many. I am sorry to hear her stay was brief and sincerely hope that other cities will appreciate her talents as much as our dear wild San Francisco does.

Yes, she is charming and amusing and will undoubtedly look like a girl long after you and I have succumbed to wrinkles.

I do hate to see our institutions move East, something I will not do. I feel that I have found a home. So much that I love is here. A trip, perhaps, when I can take the time—I am considering an Eastern tour in a year or two or three.

But you two rapscallions! On to London, twins and all... I'm sure that Arthur will buy all the theaters and you will Mesmerize their audiences. Write me from there, please. It is a place I would like to go.

My friend Sylvie—how I wish you two could meet—has been ill again. Another miscarriage. I have told her she must stop insisting on motherhood. I told her that, in fact, with her husband present in the room. He said nothing. She tells me he, too, is concerned for her health but wishes I would leave her well-being to him. Faint hope!

I have, I think, convinced her to visit me in the fall. Walter will be traveling on business and there is no reason why she cannot enjoy a week in San Francisco. I have plenty of room and enough servants for us both, and she can bring her own as well. Perhaps I can convince her to stay...and never return to Walter the Dull.

Please do not fill your next letter with veiled warnings against such a visit. One follows one's heart.

> Write to me from London, darling!
> Adela

So, Sylvie was driving Adela mad and patient Sissy Carmichael, who had saved these letters for posterity, was told not to bother her with veiled warnings! What had at first seemed a remote possibility—Adela's lesbianism—now was looking certain.

Elise found it impossible not to compare her own budding romance with Adela's. "One follows one's heart." So true, unless that one was Maiju Rittola, who would more likely bend to her fear, to the horror of whatever had happened in her past. Elise was now certain Maiju would call off the dinner. Adela's celebration of life was so different from Maiju's walled-off silences, her inward focus that seemed always to be teetering one step away from grief... she could not tolerate more pain. It was entirely possible that she was emotionally incapable of risking another relationship.

Yet however many excuses Elise advanced for Maiju's eventual retreat, she continued to wait for the phone call in a strange floating world of half-excitement; as long as the suspense continued, her date with Maiju was still on. When the hall phone rang at six-fifteen, Elise answered it in a monotone, excitement now punctured by dread. But Maiju's tone was breezy and confident, full of fun: "Are you ready? I'm eager for one of those steaks! My car or yours? Perhaps my car," she'd rattled on before an amazed Elise had a chance to answer. "You probably don't believe I can really drive."

I believe you can do just about anything, Elise thought. She quickly offered to walk the half-mile over to the Faculty House to avoid her fellow students' prying eyes ("Didja see who Elise went out with? And she was *all* decked out!").

She had dressed carefully for this date she hadn't believed she would ever have—trying for casual but sensuous. She thought she'd achieved it with her dark pants and deep wine-colored shirt topped by a handmade embroidered vest in blues and scarlets. As she walked, she told herself that she needed to calm down. For one thing she was so nervous she was about to shiver herself out of her boots. But second, since Maiju *hadn't* canceled, Elise was no doubt mistaken in thinking of this outing as a date—it was more of an off-campus meeting with a professor. Then she remembered Maiju in the car last night leaning closer and her hand starting to rise towards Elise's breast. Elise was certain that it'd happened even though the movements had been so subtle that she'd only really begun to notice them as Maiju had withdrawn. But would she not withdraw tonight as well?

Elise climbed the broad front steps of the Faculty House, roughed her fingers through her hair, and rang the doorbell. A moment later, she heard Maiju's quick steps coming down the inside staircase. She's really flying, Elise thought, and then Maiju opened the door. Her face broke into happiness, her eyes widened with delight. That's the thing about the Finns, Elise remembered suddenly from her trip. When they stop looking sardonic and all-knowing, they're as sunny and open as any people on earth, and the contrast is staggering. Just how monumental was illustrated a second later as shutters slammed down over Maiju's telltale face and eyes. She still looked welcoming, but a coolness had hidden the ebullience.

It didn't matter to Elise. She now knew without a doubt that Maiju found her entrancing. Lava flowed underneath Maiju's glacier-like exterior, a quick, coursing fire Elise had set flowing. Elise was very good in situations like this. Once she understood that she was desired, she could flirt, dance lightly around a topic, charm with the best of them. She hopped in Maiju's car with a grin, willing to be oblivious and funny until Maiju recovered her good spirits. It didn't take Maiju long. Before they were out on the river road, Maiju was laughing and telling Elise about her experiences as a badminton champion in college—she was number two seed, she said, so she always played the competing college's second-place competitor, and the result was often disastrous. If only, she said, there'd been one other slightly better player at their own school, disaster could have turned to triumph. "As a third wheel I'm terrific," she said. Then she seemed to sober, and her hands tensed so tightly her knuckles gleamed ivory in the fading light.

What happened to you? Elise wondered for perhaps the ninetieth time just that week—it was becoming a question she would have to answer. The mystery was, clearly, a tragedy of love. That's why she had avoided Elise so assiduously. She needed to stay away from her, just as Elise herself avoided Jamie. But I don't even love Jamie, she thought, though I guess my body does. She certainly didn't want to think about Jamie tonight.

They pulled up in front of the restaurant. Maiju held the door for Elise. They sat down, opened their menus. The Sportsman's Club had never looked so elegant. Elise felt she was floating. She could hardly read the list of entrees and opted indeed for the steak. Maiju kept smiling, then laughing at her smiles. She wasn't able to keep her face shuttered for long, or perhaps, paradoxically, she felt able to be more open in a public place. Nothing can happen here, Elise surmised. She's safe for the moment. Back outside, she'll close off again.

"Have you had a chance to read any of the Adela letters?" Elise had meant the question as a light conversation opener, but Maiju's expression darkened suddenly, her eyes filling with—what? Pain? Anger? Elise wished she could take the innocuous question back.

"I have read them, Elise. Please let's not talk about them tonight."

Did Maiju not want to be reminded of her role as Elise's professor? Or was there something in the letters she didn't want to think about? Elise wanted to ask her, to understand, but Maiju very deliberately changed the subject. "What exactly will you do as assistant director?"

"I talked to Ralph about that today," Elise told her. She had ordered her steak medium rare, and it arrived perfectly done, accompanied by a delicious carrot mousse and tiny red potatoes rolled on a hot grill until they'd turned brown and crusty. They both ate with relish while Elise talked about her upcoming duties.

"I can't imagine how you'll have time for anything else!" Maiju finally said. "That sounds like a sixty-hour-per-week job."

Elise smiled. "It is. That's why you have to go to college young, I guess."

Maiju's eyes grew veiled again, and for a moment, Elise thought she was angry. No, she was looking inward. Well, it had been a silly remark. Plenty of older people went to college. But best not to dwell on it and move on.

"How did you end up at Adela Honeycutt?" Elise asked, then realized she'd gone from bad to worse with that question. Maiju made a perfunctory answer, but she seemed almost hurt that Elise had asked, as if Elise should sense not only the lava beneath, but the pain too…as she had, damn it! If only she hadn't been concentrating on her earlier gaffe, she would have known what topics to avoid. So, third try is the charm, Elise… "Did you know I was a child model?" It never failed to get a response, and even though it was bad form to advance one's self as a conversational gambit, in this case it was necessary. Maiju had a past that more and more resembled a mine field, and references to the East Coast, young people, or her recent past since college were all fraught with danger.

Maiju listened to the modeling stories with growing admiration, dropping funny remarks that showed she understood the problems of being lionized too young. Where did you learn that, Elise wondered, or are you simply empathic? She knew enough not to ask. This will be a short relationship, she thought, unless we can open up some of these issues…

"You've experienced enough for an entire life already!" Maiju exclaimed. "No wonder you seem so much older."

Than who? But Elise hid her question under a raised eyebrow and a sly smile. "I feel a dozen years younger than I did at sixteen. You know how jaded you feel at that age? It's surprising you can drag yourself out of bed."

"I wasn't jaded at sixteen," Maiju confessed. "I'd fallen in love with someone in my class. I wanted to know more. I felt frightened—out of my depth."

Elise nodded. "I had a high school romance as well, with a woman who was so guilty she practically stabbed herself with steak knives whenever we made love. It was very messy."

Maiju laughed and put down her own knife. Elise knew Maiju wanted to make a joke, but each quip would probably sound more leading than the last. She settled for lighting a cigarette, studying Elise through her clear dark blue eyes. "You are very direct, aren't you? I like that about you."

"I see no reason to hide," Elise said.

"I like that too," Maiju murmured. They watched each other, Elise frank, Maiju more covert, wreathed in her cigarette smoke, as good a screen as the shadows in her office. Maiju was clever at being hidden, Elise thought suddenly, but it was something she had learned. She had once been more open, perhaps naive, comfortable only with honest forthrightness, until the terrible time had driven her into hiding. Now she admired in Elise what she had lost in herself...

"Shall we go?" Maiju asked. "Or would you like coffee and dessert?"

"Oh, no," Elise said, shaking herself from her reveries. "Let's go back." To the Faculty House, she added under her breath. She did not believe that Maiju would send her home tonight. She could not believe it, or she would not have left the table. Smiling at her own high drama, she nevertheless vowed that she wouldn't be separated from Maiju again.

Chapter Eighteen

They said little on the drive back, though Elise took a chance and stole her hand over to Maiju's thigh. Maiju caught her fingers, squeezed, and then dropped Elise's hand so she could downshift as she came around the turn to Honeycutt Bridge. Elise didn't press. She sat quietly, staring out at the dark night. It was almost November; the days were short, and the rains would be starting in the next couple of weeks. The river would become roiled, gray, impenetrable. Elise closed her eyes and prayed.

This time Maiju put her car in the back parking lot of the Faculty House. They sat for a moment, neither wanting to speak. Then Maiju reached out her hand, and when Elise took it, she was surprised to discover the fingers shaking ever so slightly, a fine tremble and Maiju's haunted eyes looked even deeper, more unsteady. Concerned, Elise swung around in her seat to face Maiju fully, and watched as Maiju's deep blue eyes shifted focus from disorientation to a hint of wildness. She began breathing more quickly. Elise bit her lip. Still neither had spoken.

"Come inside," Maiju said. If they could have left the car while staring at each other, they would have. As it was, they nearly blundered into each other trying to connect again as quickly as possible. Maiju took Elise's elbow as they climbed the back stairs. She fit her key into the lock, opened the door, and turned on the light. They stood in the large institutional kitchen that was meant to serve the various receptions and functions held at the Faculty House. The big fluorescent lights made them blink, and Elise couldn't help smiling at the incongruousness of their surroundings. "Shall I ravage you on the breadboard?" she asked Maiju.

Maiju laughed. Her eyes were clearer. She regarded Elise, and then shook her head with wonder. "You're too young."

"I'm not actually," Elise said. "Have you any brandy or wine?"

She didn't need alcoholic first aid, but she thought it might help Maiju. And it did, if only because Maiju settled down while she was scouting glasses and a bottle of cognac. Both the disorientation and the wildness, Elise mused, were too mixed with hysteria. She wanted Maiju to want her, not to throw herself at Elise as if she were leaping off a cliff. But perhaps, Elise thought, that's the only way she will be able to sleep with me. Depending on what's happened to her. Always that. Always the past.

Maiju was back to staring. She sipped at her cognac, watching Elise. Elise only sniffed hers. "Let's go to your room," she said boldly.

Maiju nodded. She turned and led the way. Her door was unlocked. Elise murmured faint surprise. "There's only three of us," Maiju said. "Me and Pearl Warner, and then Ralph Goldberg stays over here, but only on Tuesday and Wednesday nights."

Elise had forgotten that. Ralph lived in San Francisco, and he didn't like to commute. During rehearsals, he would be here more often than two nights a week. "Anyway, I don't need to lock up." She waved Elise into her room.

Her suite—a combination living room/bedroom, tiny kitchenette and bath—was different than Elise would have expected. For one thing, it was packed full. She could have pictured Maiju in a monk's cell (though admittedly the cell would be adorned with fine fabrics and ascetic but well-oiled wooden furniture), but instead Maiju had crammed her space with shelves of books, quilts, Eskimo bone and soapstone carvings, and antique furnishings. Vases of flowers filled every conceivable nook, and the whole effect was exquisite. "This is gorgeous!"

"It's what happens when you try to reduce a household to one room," Maiju said ruefully.

"But I love it!" Elise explored for only a moment, touching a gracefully arching seal, running her hand over the smooth stone. Then she turned back to Maiju, who still watched her, sipping her brandy. There was no place to sit but on the bed, which was just as Elise would have wanted it. She crossed to Maiju, set her drink on the bedside table, took Maiju's free hand, and stroked the long line of her jaw. Maiju seemed paralyzed, so Elise pried her glass from her unresisting fingers, placed it next to her own, and then leaned over and kissed Maiju gently on her lips. That woke her up. She reached her hand around Elise's neck and pulled her down firmly, guiding her until she was on her back, and then she raised her hands to Elise's face and began to kiss her searchingly, her tongue and lips invading Elise's welcoming mouth, sucking and licking, until both of them were panting, their eyes suffused with want.

"Light?" Maiju whispered.

She apparently thought Elise wouldn't like the overhead. And Elise didn't, it was true. But she would have to get up and turn it off way over by the door... Maiju accomplished the feat in a second switched on the bedside lamp, so much nicer, softer... And then Maiju was back in her arms, or perhaps she should say she was in Maiju's arms, because Maiju was so firm, so dominant in her desires now that she'd been released from her self-imposed prison. Elise reveled in this blissful surrender, this being taken, as Maiju gently undressed her, slipping off first her vest, then unbuttoning her shirt, gasping as she uncovered Elise's firm young breasts, the pink nipples standing out high and excited, more excited now by Maiju's tongue and nipping teeth, until Elise was half-growling with pleasure from deep in her throat, and she could no longer restrain her hips.

But meanwhile she was not idle. She had reached under Maiju's sweater, discovered a bra, and slid her hand around the back, unfastening it in the simple full-handed motion she'd discovered in high school. Her questing fingers found Maiju's small breasts and her high, grape-hard nipples that grew even more erect under the thrum of her caress. Then Elise was lost entirely as she felt her pants being eased off her hips, down her legs, tangled at her ankles before being dumped unceremoniously on the floor. A pillow fit under her buttocks, and her legs were thrown apart by her upward-tilted position. She cried out when she felt Maiju's mouth on her, and then Maiju's hand invaded her at the same time, rocking her from front to back, then pressing hard, pinning her to the pillow, as her clitoris sat up straight and her gasps became half-cries. She thought that she hadn't wanted to come this soon but then she was over the edge, it didn't matter, and she heard herself screaming thinly, far away, and the waves of pleasure shook her as hard as the steady pounding of the surf, stunned her, until she crawled crying up the beach, up the bed, to grasp Maiju's strong, steadying hand, a beacon in the dark, and then she lay close, her face buried deep in Maiju's shoulder.

She had begun to stir again when Maiju stopped her, fingers around her wrist: "No, there's plenty of time for that. Just rest." And she did, falling into a deep, dreamless sleep, aware that she had never felt such trust with anyone, never felt so perfectly protected or cared for.

She awoke not much later, for the sky looked the same. An unease had filtered through her sleep, scratching at her consciousness until she couldn't shove it aside any longer. The bed next to her was empty. Maiju was sitting by her window, staring at the night. Elise could only see her in quarter-view, but it was enough. The prison doors had slammed shut again. "Maiju," she called softly.

Maiju turned to her, with eyes haunted and moist. "I'm sorry," she said. "I think you'd best leave."

Elise rose blindly from the bed, rummaged on the floor until she found her pants, her shirt; she yanked on her boots. Her breasts bounced full and heavy against the rough cotton of her shirt, and she was unreasonably angry at them, the idiots, not realizing that what had satisfied them so thoroughly was now withdrawn. When she'd finished dressing, she turned with a sick dread to address Maiju. But Maiju was facing the window, her shoulders hunched in refusal. Elise stifled a wail and left, clattering down two flights of stairs to burst out on the lawn like a startled lamb at a slaughterhouse, cut from the flock to die alone.

Chapter Nineteen

She ran to her room, though that was not where she wanted to go. And once she was there, she felt trapped. She paced for minutes, sickened by the panicked sound of her own footsteps, burst into Frances's room—empty—and shot back through the bathroom, catching sight of herself in the long mirror, dressed in the outfit she'd picked so carefully to appeal to Maiju. She shrugged away her embroidered vest and then ripped her shirt down the front, tearing it off her body and dumping it into the wastebasket. Apparently Frances hadn't tried hard enough; Elise was finding it remarkably easy to rend her clothing. But now what?

Half-naked, she stalked into her room, removed her pants, and rooted through her closet—for what? What on earth did she intend to do? Never mind that. Don't think. She pulled on a T-shirt, faded jeans, a puffy bomber jacket. Her boots were the only items that made the cut. Okay, fine, so she looked hot. She didn't really want to do this, did she? She didn't. Instead she pulled out the stack of Adela's letters and pawed through them until she came to one addressed to "Dear Darling Sylvie." With fascination, she read:

❦

22 August, 1864

Dear Darling Sylvie:

I cannot believe it! Is it really true? You are coming to stay with me? Walter has agreed?

This is too wonderful. I will show you the most elegant time you can imagine. We'll eat at the City's most fashionable restaurants, see the best plays, take a boat across the Bay—will you let me buy you pretty things? Of course you will. What a celebration this will be!

I have so much to do to prepare for you, sweet Sylvie, my darling passion! Let me know the exact day and hour of your arrival. I will be at the Pacific Street Wharf, waiting for you, any day or night at any hour.

I cannot wait!

Love,
Adela

❦

3 September, 1864

Dearest Sylvie:

I shall be there, at the wharf, waiting for you with my carriage, full to bursting with happiness and expectation of sweet days to come. Only two weeks away! You will be traveling, I suspect, with a number of my colleagues returning from road tours. I envy them—business consumed my summer. And I envy all of you, to be traveling together. Tell the players you are my dearest friend and they will treat you well and keep you entertained.

We must take a steamboat ride together, you and I. Or at least a ferry. There are so many things we've never done together, for all our years of friendship. We must do them all.

Until the eighteenth then,

I remain your most devoted friend, as you know I am,

Adela

5 October, 1864

Dearest Sylvie:

Yes, beloved and gentle friend, I agree that ours was a week to remember all one's life—but do not speak as though we shall have only memories to sustain us. Please say that there will be other such times together. How good to be with you all of every day, to wine and dine and go to the theater every evening.

Why did we wait so long for such simple and precious pleasures?

I think, my sweet one, that your letter was incautious. Perhaps there are some things better left unwritten, better left secret and in the mind to cherish, more for your sake than for mine. Yet how divine to read of your love for me, to read that our days and nights of tender friendship were as joyous for you as for me.

It is harder than ever for me to bear our separate lives, to live through these solitary nights with your fragrance still hovering in the room about me, and on my pillow. If only you could come more often. I think of you constantly now, and wonder if there is a way for me to come to Sacramento this winter just for a few days.

Love always,
Adela

Oh, great! Just what she needed. Sweet, tender love, then caution on Adela's part. Things better left unwritten. But at least Adela still desired Sylvie! Desired her? She worshipped her, reveled in her, wanted her more than anything...

You're just torturing yourself, Elise thought. You've got to get out of here. Why isn't Frances around when I need her? If she were here, we could talk. It was eleven-thirty. Was that all? Her life had begun and ended in the space of five hours? Her vow—that she would

115

never allow herself to be separated from Maiju—had lasted all of two hours.

Screw-up, louse, idiot! She hurled curses at her cowering self as she slammed out the door. And then, when she saw where her feet were carrying her, where she'd known she'd end up, her imprecations redoubled. But she didn't stop walking.

She bounded up the steps of Crabtree Hall, scattering a few night-owl freshmen who gazed after her curiously. She swung into Jamie's corridor, stalked down the ten yards to Jamie's room, made a perfunctory knock on the door, and then shoved it open. Jamie was standing near her window, while on the floor at her feet sat a punked-out freshman, with spiked hair and dark red lipstick and a short skirt that barely covered her thighs. The girl sprang upright, her eyes awash in surprise and then agony as she recognized Elise, the impossible-to-best competition for Jamie's affection. And Jamie never glanced at her. Once Elise entered the room, her blue eyes were locked with Elise's green. "Go," Jamie said to the girl.

"But—" she stuttered. It had taken all her nerve to make this one small protest; she grabbed her black leather jacket and scrambled from the room, shutting the door behind her quietly.

"That was disgusting," Elise said.

Jamie shrugged.

"It's the kind of thing I can't stand," Elise persisted. "What makes you think you can run roughshod over people, over—she's hardly more than a child."

"She's old enough," Jamie said. "You'd be surprised at how old some girls like that can be." Jamie watched her. "But you didn't come here to tell me how terrible I am."

"No, I—" Elise's tears suddenly started flowing, her voice gummed up, and she ground to a halt, her breath coming unevenly as she tried to stem the tears. Jamie crossed to her more quickly than Elise had ever seen her move, enclosed her in her arms and steered her to the bed, where they both sat, Jamie rocking her gently. The tenderness was a surprise, and Elise took advantage of it by giving in

116

to her pain, letting Jamie take care of her. Jamie petted her as if she were a cat, rubbed her shoulders and arms and legs, slowly took off first her jacket, then her T-shirt, finally her jeans, then removed her own clothes in a few quick motions, as if she were shucking corn, and came back into the bed to lay her body against Elise's, pressing up against her so their breasts fit naturally and so familiarly together. Elise felt herself relaxing at the feel of Jamie's smooth strength and warmth. But when Jamie began making little noises, licking the skin at the crease of Elise's arm and the rise of her breast, Elise stiffened and pulled back.

"What's wrong?" Jamie questioned. Her voice was neutral, as if she were ready for Elise to slap her down. "What happened tonight anyway?" She raised herself on one elbow to stare at Elise. "You slept with Maiju Rittola, didn't you? I've seen you mooning over her."

Elise didn't answer, which was telling enough for Jamie. "I should turn her in, that bitch. The administration wouldn't go for it, would they, teachers fucking the students? Especially women teachers fucking students."

Elise tensed up, her heart clenching painfully inside her chest. Surely Jamie wouldn't do such a thing.

Jamie shifted her weight so she could see Elise better. "You're really in love with her, aren't you? I can't believe it. You know what people call her? The Ice Maiden. Shit, if you want to play hard-to-get games, play them with me. I'm a master at it."

I bet! Elise thought caustically. But she found herself defending Maiju. "She's not playing. She's been hurt or damaged in some way. She tries to open up, but she can't." She didn't know why she was telling this to Jamie, who was not the most sensitive person on earth, and who certainly could not be expected to be receptive in this situation. But Jamie surprised her again.

"So you're going to save her? Didn't you get enough of that with Ruth? You oughta know by now you can't save someone and be her lover too. It's unequal. You think you're helping her, and maybe you even are, but once that part is over for her, so are you."

Jamie was probably right, Elise realized. So it was doomed from the start, even if she managed to overcome Maiju's fears, convince Maiju that the risk was worth taking. But the way Maiju had looked when she'd first seen Elise that night, with that wide-open delight, or how she'd trembled when she'd touched Elise's breast and nibbled at her lips—surely all that meant something! Out of all the women Elise had slept with, only Ruth, Jamie, and now Maiju had really touched her. Being with Maiju had been so different from Jamie's rough expertise. Yes, Jamie was proficient, but her ego was all tied up with her performance, as though bed was a stage on which she excelled, her lovers characters in her play. Everything was written, acted, controlled by Jamie.

Maiju, on the other hand, had been completely focused on Elise, as if she were opening a channel between them so they could penetrate deep into the other's soul. Elise covered her eyes with her arm, realizing for the first time that while Maiju had truly wanted Elise, Jamie would never be satisfied with Elise since Jamie's salvation came from without, not within, and thus needed to be reinforced constantly. As if Jamie knew what Elise was thinking, she reached across, caught Elise's wrist in one strong hand, and pulled her arm away from her face. "Is she better than I am?"

Given Elise's thoughts, it was a pathetic question, only underscoring Jamie's inadequacy. Elise tried to free herself but Jamie was both stronger and quicker. "Stop it, Jamie," she said. She herself stopped fighting, for it was useless. She lay there, passive on the surface but inwardly boiling. They stared at each other, both grim-faced, until Jamie's eyes seemed to turn milky and she let her fingers loosen. Elise slipped off the bed and began gathering her clothes.

Jamie lay there, her arms above her head, watching Elise dress. Her words seemed to come from a deep well. "I never knew you were into games, Elise. You want Professor Rittola because she doesn't want you. She rejected you tonight, didn't she? And of course you're not interested in me because I need you. It's not a crime to need someone."

Elise shook her head helplessly. Jamie could look no further than her own tired obsessions. Unfortunately, for Maiju it apparently *was* a crime to need someone, and because of that, for Elise it was a crime to need Maiju. She was sick of it, and sick of Jamie twisting everything to feed her own rationalizations. "Thanks for holding me," Elise said stiffly.

Jamie held up an eloquent middle finger.

"Fuck you too," Elise told her softly, stepped outside the door and stood in the hall for a long moment. The same three freshmen she'd seen on her way in stared at her until one said with an ugly smirk, "Lover's quarrel?" and another muttered, "Fuckin' dykes." Elise shoved past them roughly, and they jumped aside like frightened ducks. She trotted across the lawn to her own dorm, the blood pounding through her veins. What to do, she thought, what to do. She had no idea. She stormed into her room. No one there, of course. Maybe Frances was back. She threw open the bathroom door, and there was Frances in the tub sitting on the lap of a big guy with a chest so hairy he could braid it. Even his shoulders, Elise thought, backing out of the room, murmuring apologies, Christ, he even has hair on his shoulders.

Frances appeared wrapped in a giant white towel a second later. "What's wrong?" she asked urgently. "Tell me."

Elise couldn't even talk. What could she do, where could she go... There was only one thing she knew would help when she hurt this bad. "I'm going out," she told Frances.

"Elise—"

But Elise was already closing the door. And then she began to prowl. The campus pub. No one sufficiently exciting. The library. Long closed down. She wasn't thinking straight. The dining room, with its all-night coffee machines. Deserted except for some nerdy women studying, who looked at Elise as if she were an apparition from hell. And that made it worse, made her more desperate. Back to the pub. But before she got there, she saw lights on in one of the dorm

TV rooms. Heard someone crying. Furrowing her brow, she stood there, half-pointed at the pub, half-drawn toward the crying. She could help someone, for heaven's sake, couldn't she? Take her mind off her own problems?

She entered the dorm and walked into the TV room. It was the girl who'd been at Jamie's, her red lipstick smeared now, her leather jacket draped across her lap. She looked as stunned as when she'd first seen Elise. "Jamie's free now," Elise said, and then realized how awful that sounded. Jamie had no corner on insensitivity. She shook her head. "I didn't mean to say that. I'm sorry for how she treated you, I didn't realize you were there—"

The girl was staring at her as if Elise were nuts. Well, perhaps she was. "Look," Elise said, "I'm sorry, all right?" She began to turn away, but then she heard a movement behind her.

"Don't go," the freshman murmured. She was right in back of Elise, had in fact now stepped into the doorway beside her, and Elise's eyes widened as she saw something move in the girl's face, something desperate and needy, and then she gasped as the girl reached up under Elise's T-shirt and began to handle her breasts with a rough skill that made Elise wince and then start to pant. She had never been turned on so fast, as if she'd been standing one place and then found herself somewhere else entirely. She linked her hands behind the girl's neck and yanked her forward, their mouths pressed against each other, teeth knocking together in their haste, until they were both groaning and Elise had a moment's sanity—Christ, they were doing this in a dorm TV room!—enough sanity to turn out the light and move the girl away from the doorway, far enough to collapse on the rug behind one of the sofas, where someone walking by in the hall might not spot the frantic struggle of limbs and tongues and teeth.

Chapter Twenty

Elise opened her eyes to find Frances peering at her, a worried expression on her face. When had she come home? She could barely remember. The freshman—Alix was her name—had fallen into a near-trance after their frenzied coupling behind the sofa in the living room of Carmichael Hall. Elise had stroked her ankle, a good-bye gesture which Alix acknowledged with a simple dip of her chin. You'd be surprised at how old girls like that can be, Jamie had said. Elise, remembering the need that had crossed Alix's face, hoped it was true. A flare of color came up in her cheeks as she remembered how she'd castigated Jamie for taking advantage of these women. Talk about the pot and the kettle...

But what about Frances? "Who was that anyway? Mister Hair?"

"Oh!" Frances yelped. "I forgot you'd never met him. That's Don." She looked away, out the window, anywhere but at Elise.

"But I thought—"

"He's back, sort of. Well..."

"Frances."

"Elise, don't talk to me about Don when you come back here with bright red lipstick smeared all over your face. What happened with Professor Rittola? She wouldn't use that color!"

Now it was Elise's turn to look away. Then she wanted to tell, all of it. Frances listened as she often did, with her full attention and sympathy, so it was surprising to Elise when she did not agree with her. "Maiju's bad for you," she concluded.

"How can you say that?" Elise stammered. "I just finished telling you how her face lit up, how for once I felt that someone was trying to see me the way I am—"

"Maybe you light up her life, babe, but she darkens yours. If she were really in love with you, she would never have given in to this impulse to go to bed with you. Because I'm sure she knows she's bad news."

"Oh, Frances!"

"Sorry, hon, I've got to tell you what I feel."

"But don't you think that if I could find out what happened with her, if I could get her to talk to me about it—"

"No." And then she eerily echoed Jamie's words. "You're not her savior, kiddo. You've got to come into this thing as equal partners if it's got any chance at all."

Elise shook her head. "How come you can give such good advice to the lovelorn when you're out screwing this Don guy who's really tied to Mrs. Headache?"

"It's the old saw. Do as I say. And listen, honey, I know you want to think Professor Rittola is hiding a deep, dark secret, but did you ever consider the possibility that she just has a girlfriend back East? Maybe after she made love to you, she was overcome with guilt. Anyway, think about it. I gotta go. My suggestion to you is blow all these babes out of the water, Jamie, Alix, Maiju, the whole lot of them. Go find someone new, someone completely different."

"I don't think that works," Elise said slowly, pondering Frances's theory. "I think once you're in love, you stay that way."

Frances smiled at her. "My incurable romantic," she said fondly. "Wish me luck, kid."

"Luck," Elise said, her voice faltering as she realized she was about to be left alone with her thoughts. Could Frances be right? Had Elise romanticized Maiju so much she simply hadn't recognized a woman stepping out on her girlfriend? Unfortunately, Frances's idea explained a lot: Maiju avoiding Elise at first, the undercurrent of hysteria when Maiju finally succumbed, then the quick, knife-sharp withdrawal. "I think you'd best leave." Only words, Elise told herself. Tears seeped from under her lids to streak down her burning cheeks. Words could wound as cruelly as any blade. Yet she didn't think Frances was right. Maybe she was only kidding herself, but she was certain something sinister underlay Maiju's inability to be with her, because Maiju's very soul had been compromised. Maiju had been naive, forthright, until—*it* happened. She had then walled herself off from everyone, not just Elise. And in those brief moments when she'd broken free of the darkness that throttled her, her caring, her openness, and her protectiveness had been focused on Elise alone. This was so painful to think about! She had to concentrate on something else or she would go mad. She flipped to her stomach and grabbed the stack of Adela's letters, her compulsive distraction from the real world.

❧

1 January, 1865

Dear, dear Sylvie!

Have you been agonizing about my words all this time? Read them again, sweet one. Are secrets to be secrets forever, you ask? Well, but the secret is more yours than mine. I have no husband to please, no one but myself—and you —to live for. Do not take my words of caution so to heart, but instead cherish the other words I wrote, as they express my love and pain.

We must see each other more often, or I will simply die of it. And yet, while you rail against secrecy, you say it would be too hard to meet

at your house, too hard not to be free as we
are here.

Of course, that is so. And the decision is yours.
But that means you must come here, then, does
it not?

I will not see you, otherwise, until May, in
Sacramento—when I have other reasons for being
there—unless you travel to me. I beg you to do
so, and the Devil take my words of caution and
your fear of discovery.

All my love always,
Adela

So Adela was not having smooth sailing either. Phrases
were misunderstood, becoming wounds that festered for
months. The husband was a hindrance. The two women
could only have privacy at Adela's, yet Sylvie was divided
between her wifely duties and her need to be with her lover.
Not to mention how difficult and costly it must have been
to travel then. How much easier now. Lover in Sacramento?
Two hours, tops, from almost anywhere in the Bay Area.
Call her on the phone when the hubby was gone. But there
were other problems that couldn't be solved by better
transportation and communication, problems that seemed
to have no resolution because they were unspoken.

Elise got up and paced into the bathroom, washing
away the lipstick and the tears. She could sit in her room
like a passive dolt while her life collapsed around her, or
she could confront Maiju and demand an explanation.
That's what adhering to her vow meant, taking their love-
making as seriously as it had been intended by both of
them, not consigning it falsely to the maw of one-night
stands... She stood up and actually felt faint. What would
Maiju say? There's only one way to find out, Elise, she told
herself. Courage, girl.

But all her pumping up was for naught because just
as she turned the corner to the Faculty House, she saw the
old Volvo pull out onto the road toward Honeycutt Bridge.
She waved, but Maiju most likely had not seen her, and in

any case did not stop. Where was she off to? Why wasn't she sitting in her room crying or moping as Elise was? Perhaps she really didn't care. Perhaps Elise meant nothing to her. No, she was certain that wasn't true. She'd felt Maiju's love for her, and she knew it was as strong and solid as the core from which it sprung, the core that had been compromised by whatever terrible thing had happened to her. *What terrible thing?* Maiju seemed to have so many raw, exposed nerves—wild blackberry, that's what it was like. The fruit tasted great, but the thorns were always in the way. She should take Frances's advice and find someone new, someone completely different. Torn inside, she turned around and headed back the way she'd come, her mind out on the river road with Maiju in the Volvo, imagining the beautiful line of her jaw and the rise of her thigh as she gunned the dented old car along the twists and turns of the river...

Chapter Twenty-One

The next morning there was an envelope in her mailbox. In it was a card with a photograph of an old house on it, bleached gray wood and broken windows, surrounded by gay daffodils that still made a show long after the inhabitants had left. Ice gripped Elise's stomach as she turned over the card and opened it to read:

Dear Elise: You are so wonderful that I can only tell you I wish I had met you when all was possible. I wish almost as much that I could have known how truly impossible it was for me before I caused you such pain. I suspect we would do no good for each other now; I proposed reassigning your Adela Honeycutt project to Frank Danielo, thinking that might be best for both of us, but I learned he is quite busy now, and I felt that this would not be fair to you. Since it's so close to the end of semester, if you can bear to put up with me at all, I'm certain we could cut our meetings to one or two before your paper is due in January. I have therefore canceled your normal weekly half-hour and will expect your call sometime in December to set up a final meeting. Please accept my apologies for my unforgivable stupidity. —M.R.

Elise read it three times and then she turned from the mail room, tears streaming down her face. She walked across the lawn, where she read it again. She slowly climbed the steps to her room, crossed through the bathroom, and handed it to Frances, who read it, nodded, and said, "Good. An intelligent response." Elise said nothing. She felt betrayed by everyone, Maiju, Jamie, Frances. She turned around and left the room, Frances's voice echoing in her ears.

That night she went back to the pub. Jamie was in her usual spot—that is, when she wasn't at Lulu's—surrounded by a gaggle of her soccer buddies. They were laughing and joking, but they fell silent when Elise walked in, their eyes following her as she ordered a Coke, propping an elbow on the counter before turning and insolently examining each woman in the bar. Conversations flickered and died; everyone had half an eye on Elise. Jamie tried to keep things going, but even she failed. Then Elise drained her Coke and walked out. After half a minute, three women stood up and casually strolled out after her, one of them with an apologetic shrug at Jamie. Elise had just announced she was back in action, and within hours, the whole campus knew about it.

The next month passed in a whirl. Elise threw herself into her job as assistant director for *Romeo and Juliet*; Ralph kept assuring her that he couldn't be more pleased, but she ignored his compliments. What could she tell him? That the job was saving her sanity? That she spent every night not busy with rehearsals on the prowl? She had never talked much with him about her personal life, and she didn't plan to start now. In fact, she was talking to no one, not even Frances, who kept trying to ask her out to lunch, to dinner, to somewhere, and who finally sat her down and told her in great detail of the final, absolutely final, breakup with Don, and then sat stunned when Elise murmured a few insincere platitudes and walked out without another word.

Elise had found she didn't need to speak, not even to the women she bedded. Now that the word was out, women came to her, knocking on her door late at night, sending her notes in her mailbox: "Meet me at Lulu's, 9 p.m. Monday. I'll come to you." She kept some of these arrangements and spurned others, all without discernible reason or pattern, even to herself. She rarely answered the knocks at her door, especially when they were hesitant, when the woman on the other side sounded frightened and ambivalent. Rolling over in bed to present her shoulder to the wall, she ignored the invitation. But a few times she had opened the door, wearing only her filmy nightgown, put out her hand to her caller, and drawn her into the dark room. Frances had learned to knock before she waltzed in, even if Elise had seemed to arrive safely by herself, taking her usual long bath before she crawled into bed to read. Frances had burst in just the day before to find Elise splayed out on the dark green sheets, her head thrown back, a flush spreading across her breasts and up her neck to her cheeks, half under a woman with long blond hair who was sucking on Elise's right nipple while fucking her with what seemed to be her entire hand—except that Frances ducked out so fast she couldn't really see right. Elise had only smiled at Frances's halting questions that afternoon, and reminded her that she should make her presence known next time. "But, Elise," Frances insisted, "we have to talk. Maybe I was wrong about Maiju. I mean, you can't go on this way. You should talk to her."

"I have no intention of talking to her." Elise looked up from her Italian text.

"What about your project?"

"What project?"

"Your Adela project. You have to do it. It's your semester's conference course. You *have* to do it or you get thrown out of school."

Elise's face darkened as she stared at the list of Italian verbs. "I'll do it," she said.

"Well, have you met with her? Have you called her?"

Elise shook her head.

"Elise!"

"Leave me alone, Frances," Elise said dangerously. "Just leave me be. I'll do everything in my own sweet time."

Chapter Twenty-Two

Romeo and Juliet had a three-night run the week before Christmas vacation. Elise had turned in twenty-hour days and the results showed: By the last night, after the area papers had caught wind of the professionalism of the production, the campus of Adela Honeycutt was crowded with theater-lovers from all over the Bay Area. A review—albeit printed a day after the fact—even appeared in the *San Francisco Chronicle*, making a big deal out of Ralph Goldberg, who was rumored to be "on his way East," after his marvelous successes at Adela Honeycutt and his small-scale productions in the City. Ralph, modest as usual, attributed much of the credit for last spring's *A Doll's House* and the fall's work to his marvelous actor/assistant director Elise Lemoine. A brief paragraph followed, noting that Elise had been a child actor and a model, and that she was a theater major at Adela Honeycutt—"a rising light" in the Bay Area theater community. That afternoon Elise finally let Frances take her out for lunch.

"You're famous again," Frances said. "Fame just seems to find you, doesn't it, even if you hide out from it?"

"I hardly think a couple lines in the *Chronicle* constitute fame."

"You know what it means." Frances was nibbling around her hamburger again, in concentric circles.

Elise nodded. It meant with that review in hand, and with Ralph's blessing, she could walk into any theater company in the area and get a tryout in whatever spot she chose, which translated to a major head start on every other young hopeful. She would have her chance in a shrinking market, while others just as talented would have none— and she had the added advantage of being able to slip from college right into Ralph's occasional City productions. That is, if—

"So is he really going back East?"

Elise shook her head. "I don't think so. It's just a rumor they tag on to anyone successful in the theater. They make the assumption that everyone would want to be in New York. A lot of people don't, including Ralph." Elise gnawed on a french fry. "However, I plan to pump him tonight at the cast party."

Frances had come to the exact center of her hamburger. With a wink at Elise, she plunked it in her mouth and ate it. "I don't care what I eat anymore," she said, "now that Don has left me."

"Oh, Frances!"

Frances grinned. "All right, now to other business. I continue to be worried about your stupid Adela Honeycutt project. Have you contacted Maiju?"

Elise scowled. "No," she said shortly.

"Well, I hate to tell you, it's only a few days before Christmas."

Elise had noted the same fact to herself only that morning. The success of *Romeo and Juliet* and the *Chronicle* story might help her stop procrastinating about her project. Yes, she still pined after Maiju every single day, but with her current triumphs she hoped she could create an artificial separation that would allow her to finish her paper. I am Elise Lemoine the rising light, she thought. I am not Elise Lemoine the lovelorn. I am not Elise Lemoine who runs around with other women to avoid feeling the wound of losing the one I love. I am a rising light.

She knew the glow of her successes was only temporary, and that she would once again be reunited with all her selves, including the one that hurt so much. But what Elise hoped was that the glow would blind her long enough to complete Adela Honeycutt.

When she came back from her lunch, she dug through the letters until she found the last stack, which had been waiting patiently for the six weeks it'd taken her to find the courage to finish reading them.

❦

29 April, 1865

Dear Sissy:

No, I did not know Laura Keene, for she left San Francisco shortly before we arrived. But I know she is a great friend of yours. How dreadful for her it must have been.

All of us here were shocked and stunned, of course, to hear of the heinous crime committed by dear Edwin Booth's brother John. And to have it happen at Laura Keene's very own *Our American Cousin!*

I read an account that said it was she who identified the assassin and she, may God help her, who held the dying President's head in her lap until they carried him away. Is this really true? And how is Edwin Booth bearing up?

Those here who know him well are wildly distressed for his sake, as you can imagine.

Should you see him, please tell him so.

And we were all so happy that the war was over, at last. It seems that it never is. Poor Mr. Lincoln. A martyr to our unhappy times.

    Love,
    Adela

❦

6 October, 1865

Dearest Sylvie:

It is divine to be back in gay, mad San Francisco with my little company, although being here means, unhappily, that I am away from you. As always, the highlight of our tour was the stay in Sacramento, where I was at least able to be close to you for a precious hour from time to time, when you were not helping to care for your father, not pledged to your wifely duties. But it was not enough. Never enough. Tantalus himself would die of this existence.

I am glad to hear that your father's health has now improved, but how are you? Do you miss me, truly? Tell me again. And when will you come back here for a stay? To be given only a taste of heaven is to live in Purgatory—or does that make sense? I am distraught, forgive me.

Let me tempt you to San Francisco.

I am having an enormous Christmas banquet this year, for my company and for some of the other luminaries of the San Francisco theater. You would love them all, and they would adore you, and it would be the most elegant and joyous holiday season ever. There. Now will you come?

We lead such different lives, and mine, so full of work and creativity and excitement, is such fun! But incomplete without you to share it. Try, try, try! to abandon your husband for just a few days. I have now begged you and cajoled you and promised you wonderful things, and I shall wander to another subject not so far removed.

The end of this war seems to be bringing changes to our country. I hear that there are revolutionary ideas about women and their education abroad in the land, that there are to be more women's colleges—not just normal schools and seminaries and the like—and that a university or two is considering the great heresy of coeducation. It seems that there will be more choices for the young women of tomorrow than there were for you—and certainly more than there were for me. I still regret your decision not to get your education, but perhaps you do not regret it?

Tell me this: If there were a college for women in Sacramento would you even now attend?

San Francisco attracts more luminaries every day, people I know you would adore, and who would without doubt adore you. My old friend Samuel Clemens is in San Francisco. Do you recall the writer I told you about, oh, several years ago, who was working in Virginia City? The one who calls himself Mark Twain? He is still reviewing theater and still has impeccable taste! He loves everything I do. A genius of a man who appreciates the genius of others. Too rare.

Life is good here, sweet Sylvie. Come to stay with me. I will watch over you and keep you safe from the dangers of our wild city.

All my love,
Adela

❧

3 August, 1866

Dearest Sylvie:

No, I do not believe it. You are *enceinte* again? What is your fool of a husband thinking of? What are you thinking of? And why did you not tell me of this sooner? When is the child due to arrive?

I think you should leave Sacramento immediately and come to stay with me. We have better doctors here. I shall take care of you. I shall take care of the baby, God willing. I simply cannot bear this any more, I am so worried for your health.

Shall I come to get you? What in the name of God can I do? I will come to you. I will take you away.

Only say the word and I am there.

Love always,
Adela

/

135

❧

30 August, 1866

Darling Sylvie:

He what? He forbids you to allow me to come?
And you beg me to obey? He cannot forbid me
and I do not obey him!

It is only your request that makes me hesitate,
and now I am torn between obeying your wishes
and coming to you despite them. I cannot believe
you truly do not want me there. How can I be so
sure in other things and so unsure in this, which
means so much more? I cannot help but think I
should ignore your orders and come to kidnap you.

Or send some of my troupe, in capes and
masks, to spirit you away. You must let me care
for you, as Walter has not.

I know you do not wish me to speak ill of him
but I cannot bear it! I dream of gentle embraces
and you are not here. I dream of the sweet smell
of your skin and hair and the loving gaze of your
eyes and yet you stay with him.

Still you do not say when the child is expected.
Is it soon?

Write and tell me you are well or I swear I will
dash to your side like an avenging Amazon!

My deepest love,
Adela

❧

28 September, 1866

Dear Sissy:

My darling beautiful Sylvie is dead.

She miscarried yet another time and they could
not save her.

I wrote to her begging her to come to me, or
at least to let me go to her. When I heard
nothing, I went to Sacramento. I arrived the day
after her funeral.

Her idiot of a husband would not talk to me. I bribed a servant who was close to her, and she told me all.

My beloved friend, my adored, intelligent, lovely friend bled to death.

The servant gave me a note my darling had left for me, asking that I destroy the letters she wrote to me, so that I will remember her as flesh but will not live in memories and will not be reminded of her cowardice in refusing to live with me. That same servant also found and returned to me the topaz ring I gave to her, and my letters, which Sylvie had bound with a red ribbon. I carried them away. They belong only with her, or with me. When I die, perhaps you will keep them for me?

It was only by the greatest self-control, the most iron will, that I did not shoot the detestable Walter through the head. But of course I know that would have done her no good, and there are things I can do, I think, that will grace her memory in a more fitting way, if I avoid the hangman's noose.

I have perhaps been frivolous with my fragile life. I wonder if there are not other, more serious causes to which I can dedicate my bereft heart.

I sit at my window and look out at the Bay. A steamboat docks, as it does every day at this time, a riverboat from Sacramento. I think of the time she came on a steamboat down the Sacramento River to visit me.

The river that leads to the Bay. The life that leads to death. I am devastated. I can never be the same woman you have known.

I will write to you again when I am again capable of speech.

Love,
Adela

Good god. Elise shook her head. How Adela must have cursed herself for not rushing to Sacramento. How she must have regretted that she'd not dragged Sylvie to

San Francisco. Yet she *had* insisted. What more could she have done, given the times? And to hell with the times. You cannot control the one you love, in the 1800s or the 1900s—or no doubt the 2000s either. What was that bumpersticker? "Live and let live," even if it meant letting the one you love die.

Well, certainly all the questions were answered—why Adela started her college for women, why she sited it at the Delta, midway between San Francisco and Sacramento. Elise was crying now. Why she'd left the theater and retired here to live out her days alone. Even how Sissy Carmichael had come to have Adela's letters to Sylvie—Sissy had outlived her friend and they had been part of Adela's legacy to her. So now Elise had to write it out, a simple story that might cause a big fuss... Jerks. Why should it cause a fuss? We haven't come very far at all if love between women is still so scandalous.

Her alarm blared, and she punched it off fast before she stared at it, puzzled. Why on earth had she set the alarm—the cast party! She had only twenty minutes. She tossed the letters on her bed and dashed through the side door to start a hot bath.

Chapter Twenty-Three

The pub was roaring as Elise approached along the path that twisted tortuously through the grove of redwoods which some romantic had planted fifty years earlier. The lights passed from sight behind their trunks, then reappeared brighter than before, but the racket never ceased. Reggae was blaring from the sound system, and the infectious beat had Elise skipping across the flagstones. Tonight was her night—her party.

Linda Martinez was holding court against an ugly potted palm which was supposed to add a natural touch to the dark, raunchy pub. Elise felt not a shiver of resentment. Linda had gotten excellent reviews and deserved them—she had taken direction easily, and Elise valued her talents —good actors made her job a thousand times easier. Linda now shoved through the crowd of congratulators around her, caught Elise by her elbows, and spun them both around in the center of the room. "Thank you so much!" she cried. "You were absolutely marvelous. Ralph must be so proud of you."

"You were fabulous too," Elise said, laughing as she pulled away and accepted a glass of sparkling cider from a passing friend. "I really enjoyed working with you."

"Well, I hope to do it more!" Linda knocked glasses with Elise, and flashbulbs burst in their eyes. The photographer for the student newspaper, the *Honeybee*, jockeyed for position and snapped more shots—Elise was a popular subject, being so photogenic. After a few more pictures, Elise excused herself and moved through the crowd of well-wishers to find Ralph. She had just spotted him clear across the room when she felt a hand on her shoulder—and she knew who that hand belonged to before she even turned around. For a moment, she simply paused and stared straight ahead as the music seemed to die around her and nothing penetrated, only the knowledge that Maiju Rittola was touching her, was about to speak to her. She turned and looked into Maiju's deep blue eyes, which didn't say what Elise wanted to hear, which were instead guarded and concerned. Don't worry about me, Elise thought savagely. Pity is bullshit. She was about to spin away again when she saw that Maiju was trying to shout something above the reggae and the ocean in her ears. "What?"

"I asked when you wanted to meet about Adela Honeycutt!"

It was true, they did have to meet. Now that she knew where she was going with the project, she should talk with Maiju as soon as possible. She could write the paper over Christmas vacation, and that would be the end of it. "End of the week?" Elise suggested.

"Fine. Thursday afternoon, my office, three o'clock." Maiju waved good-bye. Elise's eyes followed her out the door. Why had she come? And why show up and then leave so quickly, barely a half-hour into the party? Had she only wanted to see Elise? Of course, Ralph lived at the Faculty House part-time. They seemed to be friends, Maiju and Ralph. Perhaps she'd only made an appearance to be polite. At any rate, after weeks of not seeing Maiju, of going out of her way not to see her, of supposedly being cured by the passage of time, their encounter struck Elise just as hard, was just as exciting and painful now as it would have been at the beginning of October, and surely that was not a good sign. Elise the rising light was shaking hands with Elise the lovelorn. She closed her eyes to try to steady the shaking which had begun when Maiju touched her. Please calm down, she told herself.

Someone thrust another glass into her hand. She took a sip, expecting cider, and encountered champagne. Well, why not? Have another. Maybe it would help. She searched out one of the bottles that was being passed surreptitiously around the room. Two glasses later she was laughing again. Great, only she felt dizzy as hell. Champagne seemed so harmless, like a cherry Coke. Amazing it packed such a punch.

"You going to stand there gazing at an empty glass all night?" Ralph poured a stream of bubbly into her glass and then giggled like a kid. He was loaded too, she saw, even more than she was. Funny, she'd never seen him drunk. "I hate this place," he confided. "It reminds me of the meat market at this old Italian store that was near my folks—kind of dark and smelly and claustrophic. Wanta get the hell out of here?"

She raised her eyebrows at him. "We can't leave."

"Why? 'Cuz we're the hosts? Don't bet on it, sister. Romeo and Juliet and all the rest can carry on quite well without us; in fact they'd probably like it better. We're like parents at a junior high bash; everyone wants to turn out the lights and start necking. C'mon."

She followed him, bemused, and hopped into his very sensible Pontiac GrandAm which he insisted on driving like a souped-up sports car. "I despise Lulu's even more than the pub," he said. "So where?"

"Oh, I don't know," Elise said. "That stupid place in town? I can't remember its name. The one with all the fishing tackle in the window?"

"Ugh! Even worse. I know, the Sportsman's Club."

"Oh, that's so far," Elise objected. Her stomach had dropped at its mention. She had not been to the Sportsman's Club since her dinner with Maiju, and, in fact, intended to never go there again. And what if Maiju were there, for god's sake? What if she joined them?

"Not far at all." He spun the car around and raced out of the parking lot. "Okay, now to business."

"Business?"

"You think I dragged you out of that party just for fun? Think again. Okay." He sighed, apparently unsure where to start. "Okay. I'm a selfish guy, I admit it." Elise shook her head, but he waved her off. "Lemme tell this my own way." He turned and stared at her so long that she reminded him sharply to watch the road. "Oh, yeah," he muttered, peering ahead into the overwhelming blackness, punctured only by the twin skewers of his headlights. "My question is, how can you be so right and so wrong?"

"What on earth are you talking about?"

"Like I said, Elise, I'm a selfish guy, but I'm not stupid. I can see you dying in there. I can see you threw yourself into the play because you're running from something you can't take. And I hear the rumors. I know they don't toss people out for being gay anymore, but I also know that when you're fucking as many women on campus as you are, someone's going to notice. And when you get noticed, they find ways to shove you out you couldn't even imagine. Suddenly you're moved to a double with a roommate who smells like a sewer. All the classes you need to graduate are full. Your conference course professors are switched in the middle of your projects. And those grades you earned don't materialize. The faculty gets paid, you know. Some of them get bought as well."

Elise took a deep breath. She was suddenly very sober. "What's the selfish part?" It was a holding action. She didn't know what to say yet to his warning.

"I was selfish enough to let you bury yourself in the production. Hell, you got great results from those kids, better sometimes than I could have. You understood them in some way I didn't. You saw what Martinez was capable of. I can't believe I debated between her and Tina, because Martinez was terrific. But you made her that way. That's how I'm selfish. You made me look damned good, and I thank you for it."

"Are you going back East?" Another holding pattern. Elise to ground. I'll be landing soon.

"No." He held up his hand. "Let me qualify that. No for two years. I have reasons. Maybe after that." He smiled at her. "It's hard to resist. Anyway, Elise, what's the problem here? That kind of sexual behavior is the same addictive crap as drinking and using drugs. What are you escaping from?"

"Isn't this sort of a double standard? What if I were a sailor?"

"A lot of sailors have stunted, shallow lives. Don't mess with this. Tell me."

She shook her head. "I don't want to tell you."

He shrugged. "Okay. Okay. At least that's an answer. Be careful, Elise. That's the main message. And know that if you need help, I'm there for you. All right?" He reached over and squeezed her hand. She almost started crying. What a kind man, she thought. What a sweet, kind man. Then he flipped on his right-hand blinker and turned into the dark parking lot of the Sportsman's Club.

Chapter Twenty-Four

"So that's the story," Ralph finished. He had just regaled her with his first directorial experience, which sounded disastrous. Elise sipped at her coffee and glanced at the entrance as a man walked through. The Sportsman's Club was not nearly so magical without Maiju, without the old Volvo in the parking lot. At first Elise had been relieved, then surprised by a surge of bitter disappointment. Why torture herself about someone she could never be with? "Elise," Ralph said, waving his fingers in her face to gain her attention, "I know I'm pretty boring, but surely it's not that bad."

Elise shook her head ruefully. "Oh, Ralph! You're wonderful company. I'm just so distracted. It's—" She flipped back her blond hair, trying to gain time. He signaled to the waiter for refills on their coffee. "I, uh, had an unhappy love affair."

"Well, I figured."

He obviously wanted more than that. The waiter drifted by with a silver pot and poured more coffee with a flourish. Elise took a long while stirring in sugar and cream. Finally she said, "She didn't want to be with me."

"More fool she," Ralph commented. "Is that it?"

145

"That's it," Elise said. Her voice was constricted.

Ralph nodded thoughtfully. "This isn't the bruiser, I gather." Elise shook her head. "Good. Well, then all you need to do is get over her with some*one* else. Emphasis on 'one.' And until you're ready for that one, it's best to keep your tail clean. Something I've learned over a few hard years of broken promises and unfortunate misunderstandings and waking up with strangers. You don't need it to feel good about yourself—in fact, it has quite the opposite effect."

"I'm sure you're right," Elise said.

"And it isn't any different for gay or straight. Doesn't matter. The loneliness is the same damn thing."

"No, it's true. But not many straight people know that."

Ralph laughed. "My best pal from high school was gay. I swear, he and I had the exact same arguments with our significant others on the very same damn day. It happened over and over, it was uncanny. He and I were as alike—he died a couple years ago." He stared off into the lights of the bar, and Elise could see the tears glittering in his eyes. She felt like a dope. Other people had real problems, like dying. She should get her act together, write Maiju off, and find a woman she could love who loved her. That's what grownups did. It's what she should do. Instead she told Ralph about Adela Honeycutt and Sylvie. "So that's why she started the college," she finished. "Isn't that sad?"

"Christ!" Ralph exploded. "Maiju's your advisor on this, right? How can she stand it?" Then he immediately looked guilty.

"What do you mean?" Elise asked. Her ears had pricked up like a terrier on the hunt.

"Nothing." He closed down tight as a drum.

"Nothing bullshit." She grabbed his wrist. "What do you mean? Why should Maiju be so disturbed by what happened to Adela Honeycutt?"

"Come on, Elise, let's get the hell out of here." He hopped up and threw a five on the table. She ignored him. "C'mon!" he insisted. He stalked out of the restaurant, leaving his keys behind. She picked them up and followed him slowly.

"Ralph," she said, once they were outside. "Tell me."

He was rooting around in his pockets. "I've got your keys. Now tell me." He made a grab for them, but she danced away from him. "You shouldn't be driving anyway. All the coffee did was make you a hyper drunk."

"Fine, you drive," he said. "Now let's go."

They both got in the car and Elise sat, her hands on the wheel, the car dark and silent. "Tell me."

"What's it to you?" he asked truculently.

"I'm in love with her," she answered simply.

"Christ, I don't believe it." He pounded his fist against his forehead. "That's why she's been acting all—she's your failed love affair... Well, at least you picked a good one this time."

"Acting all what?"

"Miserable. Before that I thought she was getting over it."

"Getting over what?" Elise insisted.

"She told me in strictest confidence."

"Fine, now you break it."

"Elise."

"Ralph, you don't understand. I know she loves me, but something is preventing her from being with me. And now you know what that something is. Do you honestly think I'm going to let you get away without telling me?"

"I don't know that it's that, I mean—well, there's the whole issue of teachers not getting involved with students here too."

"Ralph, we're past the point where we can walk away. Now we're just hurting each other, and I want to know why." They sat in silence for a moment. Birds cried in the night. It was getting cold. She could hear the river lapping against the beach below them. A car started, pulled away, trailing its lights across them. They sat.

Finally Ralph started speaking. "She had someone, like Adela did, someone married, and she died in a bad way, too. Maiju's lover was killed. By her husband."

"Maiju's husband?"

"No! The lover's. Maiju and this woman had fallen in love. She was younger, your age, I guess. She'd gotten married really young, too young to know what she'd wanted. Well, she and Maiju carried on an affair for over a year, but then it got too difficult. Finally the woman said she couldn't live with her husband anymore. She went to tell him she was leaving him and why, and he shot her. Killed her. Maiju read it in the newspaper the next morning. No one knew about Maiju. No one knew who she was. There were rumors about infidelity on both sides, but the husband wasn't around to say anything either. He committed suicide after killing his wife."

Elise's stomach had dropped to her toes. "Oh, my god."

"So she left, went on to Yale, tried to start over," Ralph continued. "She said she felt like a coward, but what good would it have done to speak up? Her information wouldn't be well-received by anyone, certainly not by her lover's family. She said she stole away like a thief in the night." He paused. "Now I know what she meant when she—well, kind of blurted stuff out to me a few weeks ago. She said she was frightened. It's happening again, she told me. She said she felt cursed. I had no idea what she was talking about."

"I don't have a husband lurking around!" Elise cried. "It's completely different!" She gripped the steering wheel. "Now I see what she meant too. She said she found it so refreshing that I was open and honest about who I was. So she was with a married woman before, someone who was living a straight life." Her voice turned hard. "Just goes to show, don't play games." Then she shook her head, realizing she was being ridiculous. She was jealous of a dead woman.

"What are you going to do?" Ralph asked. He sounded frightened himself. "Besides tear my steering wheel off, I mean."

Elise released her grip and started the car. "I'm not sure," she said. "But something. This time I'm not letting her go."

Chapter Twenty-Five

Elise sat alone in her room in the dark, thinking furiously. She finally fell asleep near dawn, and when she awoke, close to eleven, she chained herself to her desk and wrote her Adela Honeycutt paper. It took her twenty hours, interrupted only twice by hamburger breaks. Strangely enough, all her anxieties had completely disappeared. She was no longer Elise the rising light or Elise the lovelorn, but simply Elise. She felt a vast relief.

At four on Sunday afternoon, after a nap, she drove over to the Faculty House. She had a feeling Maiju was not around, and indeed, the Volvo was absent from any of its usual parking places. Elise pulled her car out on the drawbridge, stopped for a moment, and looked up and down the river as far as she could see. Some RVs on the banks way up by Lulu's. Kids playing, parents yelling at them. Downstream seemed completely deserted. She hopped back in the Mustang and continued across the bridge and then headed west, away from Lulu's and the angry parents. Maiju would want solitude.

It took her forty-five minutes to find the Volvo, and she'd had to use plenty of intuition to do it. A dirt track led across a farmer's field, then circled around behind a big sycamore. The Volvo was parked on the river side of the tree, almost as if Maiju had purposely hidden it from the highway. Elise eased the Mustang nose-to-nose with the old white car and closed her door quietly. But when she appeared over the brow of the bank, she saw that Maiju had been alerted by the noise of her engine. She was standing up, her head tilted, listening. When she saw Elise, she couldn't hide the fear on her face. Then her eyes became confident up front and guarded underneath, as if she'd taken a deep breath and told herself she could deal with it, that she could ease herself out of this situation. Elise was determined to keep her off-balance. She knew she could not let herself be manipulated, or she would have lost—for both of them.

"I know about your lover," she began. Start with shock. And it worked almost too well—Maiju seemed about to faint. She wavered on her feet, and Elise caught her arms and helped her to sit down on the sand. She began to shiver. Elise pulled off her suede jacket and wrapped it around the older woman. "It's all right," she soothed.

Maiju made an ugly sound that seemed ripped out of her throat. "How could it be 'all right'?" she mimicked. "Nothing will be 'all right' again."

"That's true," Elise told her, "as long as you want it that way." She didn't know where her words came from, and she had no time to pick and choose a strategy. She simply had to forge ahead.

"What do you know?" Maiju's voice was heavy, sneering. She meant to wound, and she did.

Elise threw it off as she knew she had to. This anger was not meant for her. "She loved you," Elise said simply. "What happened was not your fault. Both of you know that. But you're hanging on to the guilt because it suits you."

Maiju tried to rise up from the sand, but Elise wrestled her down, and Maiju subsided, her shoulders hunched. Her anger seemed to have exhausted her. "Why should it suit me?" she asked, her voice now almost a whisper.

"Because you're scared to death," Elise said softly. "Because you're terrified of being hurt. Because you think you couldn't bear it if you lost your lover again." Her hands moved underneath the suede jacket, stroking Maiju's back and shoulders. She felt Maiju swallow, heard her sigh.

"How do you know so much?"

"Because I needed to more than anything, and I was lucky."

"Lucky?"

Elise shrugged. Lucky to have a friend like Ralph, but she didn't say that.

Maiju hadn't finished shivering. Elise knelt down closer to her, wrapping her arms around her. Maiju rested her lips against Elise's neck. Elise could feel her soft breath. "Ralph told you, didn't he?"

"Yes."

"I'll kill him," Maiju said. Then her lips moved with laughter against Elise's soft skin, and this time her voice was joyous. "Then I'll kiss him."

Chapter Twenty-Six

Frances was buttoning her blouse in Elise's bedroom when Elise returned from the river bank. "Elise, guess what…" Then her words trailed off as she saw Elise's radiant eyes. "Gee, what happened?"

"Something fabulous." Elise grinned at Frances. "And you?"

"Something fabulous."

"Spill it, girl," Elise said.

"Don. He's left his wife."

Elise shook her head. "Frances—"

"I have to make my own mistakes. I said to myself, Elise is going to look dimly on this. She's going to tell me I'm being a fool."

"Get serious with yourself, Frances. Life's no joke."

"Really? And when did you become an expert?"

Elise threw up her hands. "Frances, don't fight with me! Give me a hug!"

Frances did, though she was bewildered, confusedly pressing Elise to her ample breasts and squeezing her in an abstracted way. "Why are we hugging? Did you get some big part in the City or something?"

"Absolutely not. Much better. Much bigger." Elise winked at Frances.

"Bigger and better... No." Frances's eyebrows furrowed as Elise nodded her head vigorously. "But how?"

"She got unterrified."

"What about Jamie?"

"Jamie?" Jamie was about as far away from Elise's thoughts as the man in the moon.

"She came by here earlier looking for you. She talked to me about her future. She said she's realized she can't play soccer all her life."

"How perceptive."

"So she's decided to go into journalism."

"Great. Frances, why are we talking about Jamie?"

"Oh, I don't know. I guess—this is scary for me too. This is something big, isn't it? Something real."

Elise nodded. "That's exactly right. This is something real."

Elise ran the tip of her tongue across Maiju's nipple and exulted in the shiver that now no longer had anything to do with the chill. Maiju arched her body up from the sandy bank to meet Elise's lips, twisting underneath her. She was murmuring something into the fog, a chant or a promise. "What?" Elise asked. She dropped her hand down to Maiju's wetness, stroked her longingly, felt the fine hairs on Maiju's thighs standing up straight. She *was* cold, and Elise's suede jacket had become sticky from the steady dripping of the fog that crept up the river from the Bay.

"Let's go home to do this," Maiju said. "Love, yes. Pneumonia, no."

"My home's impossible," Elise pointed out, "and yours is too dangerous as well. I guess we'll have to make do with a motel until you get your place in Crockett."

Maiju smiled. "Ralph gave me the name of a discreet hotel in Benicia yesterday. I think that was his wedding present. He never would have guessed we were using a beach."

"A good beach."

"An excellent beach. But a cold one, in winter."

"But we shall return."

"Like MacArthur, we shall return. Perhaps once a year, as an anniversary celebration."

Elise wrapped her arms around Maiju's slender waist, rested her head on Maiju's shoulder, smiling at the idea of making love on this lonely beach every December, close to the holidays. She thought Adela Honeycutt, given both to sentiment and to the dramatic gesture, would approve.

▨ spinsters book company

Spinsters Book Company was founded in 1978 to produce vital books for diverse women's communities. In 1986 we merged with Aunt Lute Books to become Spinsters/ Aunt Lute. In 1990, the Aunt Lute Foundation became an independant non-profit publishing program.

Spinsters is committed to publishing works outside the scope of mainstream commercial publishers: books that not only name crucial issues in women's lives, but more importantly encourage change and growth; books that help to make the best in our lives more possible. We sponsor an annual Lesbian Fiction Contest for the best lesbian novel each year. And we are particularly interested in creative works by lesbians.

If you would like to know about other books we produce, or our Fiction Contest, write or phone us for a free catalogue. You can buy books directly from us. We can also supply you with the name of a bookstore closest to you that stocks our books. We accept phone orders with Visa or Mastercard.

Spinsters Book Company
P.O. Box 410687
San Francisco, CA 94141
415-558-9586

Other Books Available From Spinsters Book Company

❦

Bittersweet, by Nevada Barr $9.95

Child of Her People, by Anne Cameron $8.95

The Journey, by Anne Cameron $9.95

Prisons That Could Not Hold, by Barbara Deming $7.95

High and Outside, by Linnea A. Due $8.95

Modern Daughters and the Outlaw West,
by Melissa Kwasny $9.95

*The Lesbian Erotic Dance: Butch, Femme, Androgyny,
and Other Rhythms*, by JoAnn Loulan $12.95

Lesbian Passion: Loving Ourselves and Each Other,
by JoAnn Loulan $11.95

Lesbian Sex, by JoAnn Loulan $10.95

Look Me in the Eye: Old Women, Aging and Ageism,
by Barbara Macdonald with Cynthia Rich $6.50

All the Muscle You Need, by Diana McRae $8.95

Final Session, by Mary Morell $9.95

Considering Parenthood, by Cheri Pies $9.50

Coz, by Mary Pjerrou $9.95

We Say We Love Each Other, by Minnie Bruce Pratt $5.95

Desert Years: Undreaming the American Dream,
by Cynthia Rich $7.95

Lesbians at Midlife: The Creative Transition,
ed. by Barbara Sang, Joyce Warshow
and Adrienne J. Smith $12.95

Thirteen Steps: An Empowerment Process for Women,
by Bonita L. Swan $8.95

Why Can't Sharon Kowalski Come Home?
by Karen Thompson and Julie Andrzejewski $10.95

Spinsters titles are available at your local booksellers, or by mail order through Spinsters Book Company (415) 558-9586. A free catalogue is available upon request.

Please include $1.50 for the first title ordered, and $ .50 for every title thereafter. California residents, please add 7% sales tax. Visa and Mastercard accepted.